The two of them made room for me to sit beside them on the step. Suddenly our porch steps felt terrifically crowded.

"Vic," Chelsie said. "Meet Arthur Henry. This is Vickie Mahoney, my best friend."

We all looked at our shoes for a while. Mine were the dirtiest.

"Artie and I met each other at the Orange Julius stand at the mall. Yesterday.

"It was so funny," she went on. "What happened is, we ordered at the same time. . . . We both said, 'Medium Strawberry Julius' at the same time. Isn't that incredible? Then we looked at each other and both gave our order at the same time *again*. It was hysterical."

"A *medium* Strawberry Julius?" I asked, like it was important that I got the facts exactly straight. By now Artie probably thought I was the world's biggest dip. . . .

The Victoria Mahoney Series
by Shelly Nielsen

MAYBE IT'S LOVE, VICTORIA

Shelly Nielsen

Chariot Books
DAVID C. COOK PUBLISHING CO.

A White Horse Book
Published by Chariot Books,
an imprint of David C. Cook Publishing Co.
David C. Cook Publishing Co., Elgin, Illinois
David C. Cook Publishing Co., Weston, Ontario

Cover illustration by Gail Roth
First printing, 1987
Printed in the United States of America
91 90 89 88 87   5 4 3 2 1

Library of Congress Cataloging-in-Publication Data

Nielsen, Shelly, 1958—
  Maybe it's love, Victoria.

  (The Victoria Mahoney series ; #5) (A White horse book)
  Summary: As Vic enters eighth grade, she has a
number of things to think about: her grandmother's
wedding, her friend Chel's feelings about becoming
a Christian, and the mysteries of falling in love.
  [1. Grandmothers—Fiction. 2. Schools—Fiction.
3. Friendship—Fiction. 4. Christian life—Fiction.]
I. Title. II. Series: Nielsen, Shelly, 1958—.
Victoria Mahoney series ; #5.
PZ7.N5682Mab 1987   [Fic]   87-10788
ISBN 1-55513-217-0

for Julie & Roderick

1

Chelsie gave me a good hard elbow in the ribs. "You excited, Vic?"

Whizzing down the freeway, the air blowing our hair, we were finally on our way to the state fair.

"You better believe it," I said. "Corn dogs, here I come."

My little brother was wedged between us in the backseat, and at the mention of corn dogs, he popped up. "I bet I could eat twelve corn dogs, easy," he bragged. "When we get there, want to watch me try it?"

A voice up front interrupted him. "Over my dead body." Mom turned and repeated herself for emphasis. "Over my dead body, young man." Mom is very big on healthy foods; twelve corn dogs are not her idea of a balanced diet.

Matthew slouched back against the seat.

"And Terry," Mom continued, in the same stern tone, "you're driving too fast again."

Dad slowed the car a little. "Was I? Sorry. Guess I'm just anxious to get there."

She shook her head and sighed. "It's happening again," she said. "Last year I distinctly remember vowing I'd never return to the state fair, and again I find myself in the front seat of this car, speeding to the entry gate. Why?"

Dad took one hand off the wheel to give her shoulder an enthusiastic shake. "Because you're such a terrific sport."

"I'm not a sport. I'm a pushover. I get talked into this."

Dad roared with laughter, his big-guy laugh. I like his laugh. "You're not going to give us that old baloney, are you, Bobbi? You love the fair. You always love it."

"Love it? Who in their right mind loves perspiring crowds? foods loaded with sugar? crazy rides that make you queasy?"

"I do!" we all chimed at once.

Dad took the exit, squealing the tires. The centrifugal force threw all of us into one corner.

"You haven't forgotten what we talked about, have you?" Chels asked me over Matthew's head. "About my new theory?"

She had called that morning to tell me. Her idea went like this: with all the people coming to the state fair, our chances of falling in love increased by about six hundred and fifty-seven percent. She had figured it out mathematically on her calculator. I find it hard to argue with statistics like that.

"Are you sure love works that way?" I asked her now.

Her face was determined. "Love is mysterious," she said. "You never know when it's just going to walk over and bop you right on the head. The best thing you can do is be prepared. Plus keep hitting places that increase your chances."

As far as I know, Chelsie Bixler has not had all that much experience with love, but she has a way of saying stuff like this which makes you wonder. I sat back, suddenly glad I had worn my new shorts. Even if my knees did look a little knobby.

"Besides," she pointed out, "this is sure a lot easier than what Peggy puts herself through."

Peggy is a friend who is always after some guy. Last week she stopped being in love with Jeff, and now she's after a ninth grader named Ted Gibralter. As in Rock of.

"According to my calculations, Vic, today could be the day we finally meet our first real male friends: tall, good-looking, and spectacular."

"Keep it down," I hissed. "You know the walls have ears."

We both looked at Matthew, who was practically

9

giving himself whiplash trying to keep up with our conversation.

"Just peel those old eyeballs," Chelsie said, dropping her voice to a whisper.

We were getting close to the fairgrounds. All kinds of people were parading along the sidewalks. Whole families. Packs of kids. Mothers pushing baby strollers. Boyfriends and girl friends, tan and arm in arm.

Up ahead, a familiar sign—with two gigantic plastic cows poking their heads through it—welcomed us to the Minnesota State Fair.

"We're here!" Matthew shouted, bouncing on the seat.

A man sitting in a lawn chair waved us into his front yard. His handmade sign said, "FAIR PARKING AVAILABLE! JUST $3! WHAT A DEAL, FOLKS!"

"Think of it this way, Mom," I said as we climbed out of the car. "A year without the state fair is like a day without . . . without . . ."

"Mini-doughnuts!" said Chelsie.

"Pronto pups!" said Matthew.

"And deep-fried cheese curds," said Dad. "A double order."

"Argh," Mom groaned, clutching her stomach. "I feel my annual stomachache coming on."

2

"You have a very nice family," Chelsie said to me, as we followed my parents down the hot pavement toward the fair. "A little eccentric sometimes, but nice."

I squinted at them in the bright, end-of-August sunlight. They were holding hands and swinging their arms. Matthew was galloping ahead.

It was true. Mom and Dad are *known* for being nice. It's practically written all over their faces. As if he could hear what we were talking about, Dad turned around and gave us a couple of unsubtle winks. He kept winking until we winked back.

"Maybe it has something to do with the way they feel about God," Chels added. "Now that I'm a

Christian, too, maybe I could act more like them."

Just a couple of days ago Chelsie came with me to youth group, and all of a sudden she became a Christian. I've been praying for her for *years*, and just like that she went ahead and did it.

It was during the group prayer. Our youth pastor asked for hands ("Is there anyone here who'd like to know more about Jesus?") and she raised hers. I didn't look, of course, since I was supposed to be praying and all, but I could feel her raising her hand. And afterward she went into another room with the youth pastor and some other kids, and when she came out she said, "I did it, Vic." It was a real shocker, all right.

"Trouble is," Chels was continuing, "I'm new at it. So how do you do it? Like this?" She grinned an enormous grin. The sun flashed on her metal braces.

"I don't think so," I said. "I think it's more natural. Not so put on."

Chels stopped smiling. "I sure hope I get the hang of it soon. School starts next week, and I want people to see I've changed."

We split up to pass by a wide group of teenage boys walking side by side in identical jeans and white T-shirts, and hurried to catch up with Mom and Dad, who were already waiting for us at the entry gate.

"You'll help me, won't you, Old Vic?" Chels asked. You've been at this longer than I have.

"You'll show me how to act like a Christian, won't you?"

"Sure," I said, even though the thought gave me this sudden itchy flutter in my stomach. It was a big responsibility being someone's role model. Especially since sometimes I'm not even sure how *I* should act. I sent up a silent prayer. *You heard that, Lord, didn't you? Help me know what to do.*

Then Matthew came dashing back and latched onto my arm. "Hurry up, you guys," he said, trying to tug me faster. "We've got to plan what we're doing first."

"Where to?" Dad called as we approached.

We huddled in a circle, thinking.

Mom called out the first idea. "The dairy building! There's always lots going on there."

"Or the midway," said Matthew. "We could go on a ride. The Hammer spins you around and around and upside down."

Dad gave him a pat on the back. "Maybe we could start with something a little less traumatic, huh? Let's let your mother choose, because she's being such a good sport."

At the dairy building they were already doing a butter sculpture, and there was a crowd around the refrigerated glass case. Inside the case a girl sat posing. You'd have to see it to believe it. She was a princess of something or other; I couldn't read her sash. A woman wearing a big parka and thick gloves was carving away at a huge block of butter.

13

Everything inside the case rotated slowly. They both looked like they were freezing, but the beauty princess kept the big smile plastered on her face.

Chels and I weaseled up front for a closer look.

"I'll bet *she* never has to worry about people falling in love with her," I muttered. The princess had wild dark curls down her back and eyelashes about an inch long. "Maybe if I wore a whole lot of mascara I could get the same effect." I doubted it.

"Yeah, but she probably spends her whole life going from contest to contest. How would you like to play accordion solos and parade around in a .bathing suit all the time?"

"Ugh. Or have my head carved out of some slab of butter. I guess you're right."

We watched silently for a minute. Suddenly I became aware of some voices behind us. Familiar voices—my dad's and my brother's.

"Well, it can't be the world's easiest job to make a sculpture out of a block of butter." That was Dad, talking in an uneasy, hushed-up tone.

"But it doesn't look anything like her!" said Matthew. Loudly.

The artist kept working. She peeled away curls of pale butter, making thick waves that didn't look much like hair.

"Look at that huge-o chin," Matthew squawked. "And the neck! That neck is like a tree trunk!"

Now people turned to stare.

"Hey, pipe down, Old Boy," said Dad.

14

"That old slab of butter doesn't look like her at all," said my brother in the loudest whisper ever. "It looks just like Frankenstein!"

Chelsie clapped a hand over her mouth.

"Matthew!" my mother said.

"What'd I say?" Matthew said.

I kept facing forward, but when I sneaked a peek over at Chelsie, our eyes met. Suddenly we both started to snicker. Then Dad let out a guffaw. Mom snorted. Pretty soon we were all choking with laughter. The people around us stared in surprise, and we charged through the crowd to the exit.

"Matthew," said Dad, trying to look stern when he finally caught his breath, "we need to have a serious talk about good manners in public places."

"One thing is sure," Mom said. "We'll never be able to set foot in the dairy building again. And I had my heart set on a double-dipper ice-cream cone. Chocolate."

"Really?" said Dad, one eyebrow up. "But ice cream is loaded with sugar. Maybe you forgot."

"Well—"

"Look, there's a stand selling fresh fruit. Mmm, delicious, and so good for you. Come along. I'll buy you some."

Mom looked disappointed, but she went along peacefully.

They returned with pineapple chunks on a stick. "You kids want some?" Dad asked.

"Pass," said Chels. "When I come to the fair, I

eat strictly junk. I'm gonna hold out for cheese curds. Let me know if you see a stand."

"Gross," said Matthew, crossing his eyes and sticking out his tongue.

"Okay, gang," Mom said, putting a restraining hand on Matthew. "Let's check out the livestock."

"You're a wonder, Matthew," Chelsie said to my brother. "You're definitely one of a kind."

"Is that good?" he asked suspiciously.

I used to think that chickens came in only one color, just plain white. But in the poultry building there were all kinds of wild-colored chickens on display in wire cages: grey and tan ones, pure black ones, speckled, spotted, and striped ones.

"Starting now," I announced when we got to the end of the third row, "no more baked chicken for me. I can't be responsible for the murder of innocent chickens. I couldn't live with myself."

"I'm with you, Vic," said Chelsie.

I smiled at her. It's great to have a friend who understands things.

Dad gave a long whistle. "If you think this is bad, wait till we get to the cattle barn. One look in those big brown eyes, and you'll be a vegetarian for life." He paused. "Maybe I *should* cook more meatless dishes." Dad is a restaurant chef, and he likes to try weird new foods out on us.

We stopped for snow cones. Plus Dad got some warm, salty popcorn which Matthew dug into as though he hadn't eaten in a month. (Chelsie

16

couldn't have any on account of her braces.) We were on our way to the cattle building, when Chels suddenly yanked on my arm.

"It's working, Vic, it's working," she said.

"Ouch. You're pinching my elbow off. What's working?"

"My theory. My love theory. Right now there's a guy giving you the eye."

I looked around. There was a guy looking in our direction, all right. His mouth was slightly open. He glanced away quickly.

"I'm not sure, but I think it was an accident," I said.

"Glance over again. Not now! Okay, *now*. See if he's still looking. Act casual."

He *was* still gawking, and suddenly I had this creepy feeling that other people were looking at me, too. They were all focusing on my—chest. I looked down. There was snow-cone juice on my shirt.

"Oh, great!" I said, turning raspberry-colored.

We took off after my family, but I kept my arms crossed.

Our legs were finally worn out; even Matthew was dragging. We made the long walk to the car in the dark.

"This is absolutely my last year at the fair," said Mom. "Absolutely my last."

"I can't believe you ordered cheese curds," Dad

said, shaking his head in pretend disgust. He unlocked the doors.

The drive home was peaceful. Matthew slept up front. The streetlights flashed into the car as we zipped along.

Chels said something so quietly I had to ask her to repeat it. "I can't believe it," she said. "That was our one big opportunity, Vic, and we blew it. We'll be the only girls in eighth grade without boyfriends."

That was depressing. In seventh grade boyfriends had been no big deal, but in eighth grade you were probably laughed out of school if you didn't hang around with some good-looking guy.

"Don't worry, Chelsie," I said. "You'll find someone."

"What makes you so sure?" she asked glumly.

"Well, for one thing, you're getting your braces off tomorrow. Guys will probably be lined up outside your door by the time you get home."

"Think so, huh?" she asked.

We drove along in silence for a while.

"So much for our big chance," I heard her mutter.

3

I was dreaming about the Tilt-O-Whirl. Chelsie and I were strapped into one of the spinning teacups, and every time the ride finally came to a stop the jolly ride operator would shout, "One more time!" and start it up again.

A knock on my bedroom door interrupted my dream.

"You awake?" called a cheerful voice.

If there's one thing that gets me in the morning, it's cheerfulness. Some people are not morning people—me and my mom, for instance. Mom says that she doesn't really get steamin' until eleven o'clock or so. The older I get, the more I understand what she means.

"You awake?" the voice called again, louder, and then the door squeaked open. I didn't even have to crack an eye open. I knew who it was: Isadora. My grandmother.

"I'm asleep," I said. "I'm sawing logs."

That didn't stop her. "Well, I'll be. You *are* still in bed! Your brother *told* me you were, but I had to come see for myself. For goodness' sake, girl, you're going to miss the whole day. And it's a beautiful day, too. Toasty and blazingly bright. Get up. I want to show you something."

I groaned and sat up. Isadora stood at the end of my bed, holding a large paper sack. I blinked at her, and she slowly came into focus. Isadora is not your typical-looking grandmother. For one thing, now that her hair was growing out, part of it was bright fox red and part was her natural color, silver gray. Not your typical L'Oreal TV commercial effect. Plus she is young looking for her age. And thin.

"You look terrible!" she said. "What did you do to yourself at the fair yesterday?"

"My stomach isn't the greatest," I admitted. "Near the end, Chelsie and I split a batch of salt-water taffy, and I think it was a mistake. Mom *said* I'd regret it."

Isadora rustled the bag. "Well, I have something here that will put the sparkle back in your eyes. Take a look at this!"

With a whoosh she swung out a flash of fabric so

that it spread over me like a magic carpet.

"What is it?" I asked, taking a close look at the mustard-colored material with black bull's-eye shapes all over it.

Her eyes were all shiny bright, and her cheeks were round and smiley. "This is the material I've chosen for your maid-of-honor dress."

For a second I was stunned. "For—my dress?"

Isadora was getting married to Harold Wilkes in November, and she had asked me to be her one-and-only bridesmaid.

"Yes, for your dress, silly," she said. "Don't you love it?"

"It's very bright," I said.

"Yes, isn't it? That's what I love about it. Don't you think it's . . . unexpected?"

It was unexpected, all right.

"Aren't most bridesmaid dresses lavender or pink or blue?" I asked. I said it delicately; I didn't want to hurt Isadora's feelings. But I had this image of myself coming down the aisle at the wedding and people falling right out of their pews laughing when they saw me.

"Lavender, bah! Who wants to be like everyone else? I want your dress to have spunk galore."

If I stared at the bull's-eyes for long I got dizzy. "What did Mr. Wilkes say about it?" I asked.

"He was a little dazzled at first, but he's a dear. He said he'd live with it if he could wear a string tie and a plaid shirt."

21

Oh, boy. This was going to be some wedding.

"Get out of bed, sweetie. Your mother has promised to help me take your measurements and cut out the pattern pieces."

I'd call Chelsie. She'd have words of wisdom. And November was still two months away; that gave us time to come up with a plan. And at least none of my friends would be invited to the wedding to see me march down the aisle. Old Bull's-Eye Mahoney.

"See you downstairs," Isadora said, taking her rumpled paper bag and pulling the door closed behind her.

4

Chelsie and her mom were out front weeding when I squeaked up the driveway on my bike. Mrs. Bixler looked out of place. Now *my* parents love to weed the lawn; they do it all the time. Sometimes I think they like anything that will get them into their grubbiest clothes. But Mrs. Bixler is not the grubby type, and here she was kneeling in the grass near the shrub garden. In white pants, no less.

"Hello, Victoria," Mrs. Bixler said as I squealed to a halt. "What a nice outfit you're wearing." Mothers are always saying stuff like that.

"Vic!" said Chelsie. "Wait till you hear what happened."

I snapped down the kickstand and ran over to

where she was working.

"You know Susie Laplorden, don't you?" she asked.

Susie is the kind of person everyone knows. She was an eighth grader last year, so it's not like we were best friends or anything. Eighth graders do not associate with seventh graders. But I had heard rumors that she was going to try out for freshman cheerleader.

"She just walked by here with Justin Brookes," Chelsie continued, waving a weed around excitedly. "You know him, don't you? He's pretty cute. Well, there wasn't much space between them, know what I mean? They were close! They might have been holding hands, but I'm not absolutely, positively sure. I didn't want to stare."

"They looked too young to be holding hands," interrupted Chelsie's mom. She stood examining her gardening gloves for holes.

"Oh, Mom." Chelsie sat down on the grass, impatiently. "Susie's in the ninth grade. That's old enough to *date*. Right, Vic?"

Contradicting someone else's mother is not a healthy habit. I didn't say anything.

"Well, in my day," said Mrs. Bixler, "ninth grade girls and boys didn't go out on dates."

I could see the disappointment spreading across Chelsie's face. If ninth graders were too young to date, that left little hope for eighth graders.

But Chels suddenly gave me a whap on the leg

24

and said, "Anyway, I'm glad you showed up, Vic. There are plenty of weeds for everyone. Wouldn't you just love to help out? I was about ready to start on the driveway. Come here, you little monsters."

I followed her over and put some muscle into pulling weeds out of the cracks in the driveway without snapping their roots.

"Guess what?" I said. "Isadora picked out bridesmaid material, and it's really—something."

" 'Something,' huh? Horrible, you mean."

You can't put one over on Chelsie.

"Yellow with black bull's-eyes," I said miserably.

Chels started laughing. The laughter built until it knocked her over, and she just sat there on the cement, laughing her head off.

"Very funny," I said.

"It really is." She wiped a tear out of her eye. "No, sorry. Let me think. There's got to be something we can do." She let her face go all serious; then she looked up and smiled. "Wear a shawl," she said. "We'll find a great big one, extra-large size."

"The pattern *comes* with a shawl. We're making it out of the bull's-eye material. Mom and Isadora cut out the pieces this morning."

Chels couldn't keep the smirk from sneaking up again. "I'm getting a front-row seat to this event. That's all I can say."

I stuffed as much sarcasm into my voice as I could. "Thanks loads for all your help."

25

Chels positioned herself above a bushy weed and pulled. "Iz is unique; she's an artist. We should have known she'd never go with anything humdrum."

Mrs. Bixler called to us. "That's enough for today, girls. Time for a cool drink, then off to the orthodontist." She looked great—tidy enough for tea with the queen. I, on the other hand, was smudged and dusty.

Inside, Chels and I sat practically glued to the air conditioner. The vent blew right at us. It was delicious.

Chels closed her eyes and took a long icy drink of her mom's homemade punch. "This is the life," she said. "Hard to believe we'll be back in school by this time next week."

"Don't talk about school," I said. "Part of me is excited to get back and see what everyone's been doing all summer. But part of me wishes summer could go on forever."

"I know," she said.

We went upstairs, and I watched Chelsie brush her teeth, which can be really sickening if you let yourself think about it. One time I watched Matthew spit into the sink and I almost threw up. But Chelsie and I are pretty close friends.

We sat on her bed and she showed me how she had figured our chances for meeting guys at the state fair.

"My first experiment was a failure," Chels admitted, turning off the calculator with a little beep, "but the way I look at it, we have other golden chances coming up. The orthodontist's office, for one."

"Except all the guys there have crooked teeth," I pointed out with a laugh.

"Or tin grins," added Chels.

She leaped up and started flinging clothes around. She found some clean jeans, and hopped into them. "Today's the great awaited Braces-Come-Off Day," she told me. "Want to ride along and watch? You can be the cheering section."

"What are best friends for?" I dialed my house to ask permission. Matthew answered.

"Say 'pretty please,'" he said. "Then you can talk to Mom."

"Matthew, cut it out."

"Say it."

"Pretty please. Now give the phone to—"

"With hard boiled eggs on top."

"Matth-ew."

"I'll give Mom the phone right after you say 'pretty please with hard-boiled eggs on top.'"

Finally I heard an annoyed voice in the background saying, "Sonny, I've had just about enough," and he handed over the receiver.

"Hi, Mom," I said. "Chelsie wants me to go with her to the orthodontist's office to watch them take her braces off. Say yes. Please?"

"Okay, but be home as soon as you can." She

sounded dead tired. "This is supposed to be my day off, and your brother is on the rampage. I need a reprieve." Mom is a counselor at a senior citizens' residence, and sometimes she says her job is a piece of cake compared to the ordeals at home. I try to be sensitive about that.

"You're absolutely my favorite mom," I told her. "I'll be home before you know it."

5

At the orthodontist's office, I was reading a magazine so old the cover story was about the upcoming movie, *E.T.* Mrs. Bixler sat across the waiting room, buried in a pamphlet called, "Great Habits for Good Dental Hygiene." I heard someone say, "Hey, Vic, buddy," and when I looked up, the sunlight from the picture window blinded me. Chels was almost right under my nose before I saw her.

"Hey," she said softly again, keeping her teeth covered with her lips.

"Okay, let's see," I said.

She grimaced self-consciously, and finally the smile burst right out. Her teeth were beautiful—as

29

straight and shiny as piano keys.

Mrs. Bixler got up from her seat. "This calls for a celebration," she said. "Break out the caramel apples, popcorn, and carrots." Then she looked surprised at herself. She's not usually much of a kidder. I laughed out loud, and Chelsie yukked it up too, showing plenty of tooth.

A doctor in a white coat emerged from the office and shook Mrs. Bixler's hand gravely. "Excellent response to the treatment," he said. This is how doctors talk. "We're very pleased with the results."

"Thanks to your expert care," said Chelsie's mom formally. "Herbert and I appreciate the time you've taken with Chelsie's braces." Chelsie's dad, Herbert, is an orthodontist who works at the same office. He couldn't do Chelsie's orthodontic work, probably because if it's your own kid you couldn't bring yourself to tighten the wires enough. Right at this very minute, however, he was probably in the back cranking up the pressure on some poor kid's teeth.

"Thanks, Doctor Brandon," Chelsie said. "See you."

"Don't forget your next appointment," he advised her in his best doctor's voice. "We'll fit you with a retainer." Then he relaxed. "Knock 'em dead in eighth grade, kiddo." It wasn't the kind of statement you expect from a dignified doctor. He headed back into the examining rooms, waving.

At the door we paused politely to let someone

pass. It was a guy, fourteen at least, followed by a woman who was probably his mother. Chelsie gave the guy a shy smile as he went by.

In the car all three of us crowded into the front seat. It was cozy.

"I've been thinking about the wedding," Chels said, as we pulled out of the parking lot. "The whole time Dr. Brandon was working on my teeth, that's what I was thinking about. And I have a plan."

"What are you waiting for?" I asked. "Spill your guts." Then I wanted to die. What a crude thing to say; it's something I picked up from Matthew, and not the kind of phrase you want to use in front of Chelsie's mom.

But Mrs. Bixler surprised me. She didn't react at all. She just said, "Harold and Isadora's wedding? What about it?"

I explained the whole situation, bull's-eyes and string ties and all.

"Hmm," was all she said.

"Want to hear my plan?" Chelsie started talking fast, like a drill sargeant. "You get involved with the wedding planning, see. You infiltrate. Then, when you've got their confidence, you subtly influence them—you know, give advice. That way you keep their plans under control."

"It's an idea," I said doubtfully. Isadora and Mr. Wilkes didn't seem like easily influenced types.

"Maybe," Mrs. Bixler said gently, "maybe you're approaching this the wrong way. Maybe wearing a unique dress isn't the end of the world."

What I wanted to do was explode: "Oh, sure. Easy for you to say. *I'm* the one who has to put it on and parade around in front of the whole world." But of course, I didn't.

"Even if the dress is a little on the unusual side," she said, "keep in mind that weirdness makes the world go 'round." Then she burst out laughing. "That's a good one. I'll have to remember that." She was on a real humor roll today. Then she became her serious self again and concentrated on the road.

We stopped at a cafe for coffee. It felt very elegant just to be drinking coffee and talking. We didn't even order any food. The three of us sat at a round table. There were tiny pink sprigs of flowers in a vase in the center. The air smelled of cinnamon.

"We all have our own tastes," Mrs. Bixler said, picking up the conversation again. "Perhaps tolerance is the key. We should be willing to accept each other's eccentricities."

"And be a little weird ourselves," said Chelsie, flashing her million-dollar smile. "The stranger the better."

"Well—" said Mrs. Bixler, but she was smiling.

I took a sip of hot coffee. I didn't feel like smiling at all.

6

Isadora gave a yank to the hem of the bridesmaid dress and looked up from where she was kneeling on the bathroom tile.

"*Victoria*, I'll never get this done if you keep moving around. I've repinned this hem three times and it's still not straight."

"Sorry," I said and concentrated on standing very, very still. But I couldn't help fidgeting. The dress made me edgy. It made my feet itch.

"Just give me another ten seconds," she said, "and it'll be perfect." Isadora adjusted her reading glasses and frowned again at my hemline.

Mom appeared in the doorway.

"This may be a stupid question," she said, "but

why are you doing dress alterations in the bathroom? And why is Victoria standing on the toilet?"

"Any law against it?" Isadora asked cheerfully. It was hard to understand her because of the pins between her lips.

"It just seems a little odd."

"It's the best place to mark a hem. You've got bright light, a mirror, a toilet to stand on. Didn't I teach you that? Goodness, what kind of mother was I?"

So far I had avoided looking at myself in the mirror above the sink, but now I looked up and groaned softly. Isadora and Mom didn't seem to notice. They were too busy squinting at the dress.

"I think it's a little crooked on the left side," Mom said. "A quarter inch or so."

"Really? Pass me the pincushion."

This is something I have noticed about adults, my parents in particular. They can see that a hemline is crooked and not even notice that the real problem is that the dress is hideous.

"I'm done," Isadora said, jamming one final pin into the fabric and smacking her palms together. "What do you think?"

I hopped off the toilet. She was so excited I didn't have the heart to tell her I thought I looked like a gigantic bumblebee.

Mom said something nice about the pretty fall color and my, wasn't that hemline just perfect. She started out the door. "By the way, Vickie, I came up to tell you that Chelsie's waiting out front for you."

"Great," I said. "Best news I've had all day. Could you tell her to come on up? I'll be in my room, changing."

Mom had a strange look on her face. "Maybe you should just go outside and meet her."

"How come she's outside?" I asked. "Usually she just barges right upstairs."

Mom hesitated, mysteriously. "She has this certain . . . friend with her."

"Who? Old Peggy? I haven't seen Peggy in ages."

"No. It's a male friend. A boy. A guy. Of the other gender. Get my drift?"

Be cool, I thought. *Act casual*.

I shrugged. "I guess I'll get dressed and go outside." Then I turned around and trudged up the stairs to my room.

The whole time I was changing—carefully, because of the pins—I was imagining who the mystery guy could be. Her cousin from Duluth? I had met him once. His name was Roy and he was a bra snapper. The whole time I was over at Bixlers' house he was trying to sneak around behind me. Or maybe it was the little kid she baby-sits. Sometimes my mom likes to joke around. She might actually tell me there was a *guy* outside when it was really just a little kid, which doesn't qualify at all. I tried to peer out of my window, but you can't see the front door from my window. All I could hear was giggling.

At the front door I paused, took a breath, and turned the knob.

"Hi, Vic. What took you so long?"

Chelsie was there on the front steps all right, and sitting right next to her was a real, live guy.

The two of them made room for me to sit beside them on the step. Suddenly the porch steps felt terrifically crowded.

"Vic," Chelsie said. "Meet Arthur Henry."

Arthur Henry, I thought. *I like it. Has character.* And it was about a hundred times better than some fakey macho name like Ted Gibralter or something.

"Hi, Arthur Henry," I said. "What's your last name?"

"*Henry*," said Arthur Henry, piercing me with the old eyeballs. "My last name in Henry."

I could have croaked.

"And this is Vickie Mahoney, my best friend," Chels cut in. "She goes by Vic."

"Hi," said the guy, kind of loudly. "Call me Artie." He was redheaded. He had nice hair, brushed back, and blue eyes. I guess you could say he was good-looking.

"Right," said Chels. "Call him Artie. I thought you two should meet. You know . . . sort of get acquainted."

We all looked at our shoes for a while. Mine were definitely the dirtiest.

"Artie and I just met each other," Chels said after a couple minutes. "At the Orange Julius stand at the mall. Yesterday.

"It was so funny," she went on. "What happened is, we ordered at the same time. The clerk came over and looked at Artie first and then me, and paused, and we both started ordering. We both said 'Medium Strawberry Julius' at the same time. Isn't that incredible? Then we looked at each other and both gave our order at the same time *again*. It was hysterical."

"A *medium* Strawberry Julius?" I asked, like it was important that I got the facts exactly straight. By now Artie probably thought I was the world's biggest dip.

"Right," said Chelsie, nodding. "Medium Strawberry Julius."

Artie didn't say anything at all. He just tapped his shoe on the sidewalk as if his foot were a pogo stick. He was probably itching to get on his skateboard, which was parked on the grass, and speed away. "You live here?" he asked finally.

Now Artie had said something stupid, too. We were 1-1. A blush eased into his cheeks, and I cut in quickly so he wouldn't feel too embarrassed for long.

"Yeah, my parents are fixing it up. They're fix-up fiends. You know, the old paintbrush-sandpaper trick." He looked interested, so I kept talking. "They've been teaching me stuff. I can wallpaper

37

like crazy. Stripes and everything."

Artie said, "I have this dumb basketball player wallpaper in my room, you know, from when I was a kid? And I started putting up posters and before you know it—bam!—there's not an inch of basketball wallpaper showing anywhere."

"Putting up posters would sure be easier than pasting up all that drippy wallpaper," I said. "But I don't think my parents would go for the idea."

"I'm not allowed to hang posters in my bedroom," said Chels, sighing. "Mom says tacks mar the wall. You know, leave holes in it."

"Use tape," Artie suggested.

"Pulls off the plaster," Chelsie said. "All I get on my wall is this dumb painting of a poodle."

We laughed wildly at that. I've seen the picture, and it is kind of dumb.

Then we started talking about school and teachers and things kind of loosened up. Chelsie was in a superterrific mood. She laughed at everything Artie and I said. Her teeth looked great.

We were going about a mile a minute when a familiar car pulled into the driveway.

"Hi, Mr. Wilkes," I called out.

He came up the sidewalk with a jouncy spring in his step. His hair, which is white, was trimmed and neatly combed. He always smells wonderful after a trip to the barber.

Chelsie says that when love agrees with someone, it shows in the face: another of her theories

38

about love. In Mr. Wilkes's case, I guess it's true.

"You look dashing," I said.

Chelsie introduced Artie, and they shook hands, as if they were PTA officials or something. Mr. Wilkes gave Chelsie a sly look that asked, "This your boyfriend, Chelsie?" I was glad he didn't say it aloud. That would have been a disaster.

"I dropped by, looking for Cupcake," he said, letting go of Artie's hand. "She around?"

Cupcake? Mr. Wilkes had been getting extremely mushy lately.

"Isadora's inside," I said. "Just walk in."

But Mr. Wilkes didn't seem to be in a hurry to go anywhere. He planted himself on the sidewalk, leaned against the railing, and shoved his hands into his pockets. "I was down at the senior citizens' center, and all of a sudden I started thinking about her. And, don't you know, I just had to jump in the car and come find her. Yes, sir," he said, jingling change in his pocket, "love's a powerful amazing thing. One minute you're just an old widower, living alone, and the next minute you're a lovesick schoolboy driving up and down streets, combing the town for the love of your life."

Chelsie nodded, blushing. "I've heard that can happen."

Mr. Wilkes gave Artie a wink. "That ever happen to you, Art?"

I leaned down to tie my shoe. It was laced up tight, but I tied it again anyway.

"No, sir," said Artie politely. "I guess not."

Mr. Wilkes lifted his index finger. "You mark my words—" he began, and we all held our breath, afraid that he might say something terrifically embarrassing about when we grew up or something. But he didn't. Instead, he just stood there, all smiley and sleepy eyed. He looked the way my cat, Bullrush, looks when he's found a sunny spot to snooze in. Probably Mr. Wilkes was thinking about Isadora, the love of his life, again.

"Well," said Artie, "I guess I should get going now." He said he had to go to some practice or other. I forget what kind of sport.

"It's been a genuine pleasure meeting you." Mr. Wilkes shook his hand again.

We all said good-bye.

"So long, Artie."

" 'Bye, Vic."

"See you, Artie."

" 'Bye, Chelsie."

After he headed off across the lawn, with the skateboard under his arm, he didn't wave or anything. But he did kind of look back over his shoulder and grin.

We paused uncomfortably. Here is what I was thinking, and it was something so crummy I'm glad no one could read my mind: *If only Mr. Wilkes hadn't shown up, we wouldn't have had to stand around talking about love and being embarrassed.*

"Hope I didn't scare the young man off," Mr.

Wilkes said, interrupting my thoughts. His face was kind of slouched and slack, and he was waiting to see my reaction. I got up off the step and put my arm around him. Or *almost* around him. He is kind of wide across.

"You were great," I said, surprising myself— because it was true. "Artie liked you."

"I wasn't too—pushy?" he asked.

"You were yourself. That's important. That's what everyone says, anyway."

"Astute observation, Victoria, my girl. Say, have I told you two, lately, that you're my favorite friends? Barring Sweetpea, of course."

Sweetpea? Good grief.

He climbed the steps, holding the rail. "Guess I'll go inside and see what's cooking. Catch you two later."

After the door clicked shut, Chels said, "Vic, I've got to hand it to you."

"Why?" I sat down in my old spot on the step. It was still warm.

"You were so nice to Mr. Wilkes. You could have let him have it, but you didn't. I could tell you were kind of uncomfortable with him around."

"*Me?*" I said. My voice was a squeak. "What about you? You were so nervous you were made of ice."

She got a kind of distant, snooty look. It's a look that can be really irritating if you're in a certain kind of mood. "*I* wasn't nervous; I like having Mr.

41

Wilkes around. He's . . . refreshing." It was the kind of word parents can use, but it sounded phony coming from her. "Anyway, stop getting me off the subject. I was trying to compliment you."

"Okay," I said, putting my arms around my legs and leaning my cheek against my knees, which were a trifle bony. "Go ahead and compliment me."

"I think you handled it real well. I—" Her face suddenly had a twinge of sadness in it. "I wish I could be more like that."

We were silent. I kept thinking that anything I said would sound preachy and superior. A squirrel came hopping delicately across the street and up the sidewalk. It hesitated, staring us down. Its fluffy tail twitched. Finally it hightailed into the bushes.

"It's hard to be nice sometimes," I said.

"It looks easy."

"It's not. But it's a good idea to try."

"Yeah," she said. "I bet Jesus was real nice and polite to everyone. He would have been pleasant to Mr. Wilkes, even if Mr. Wilkes *was* saying embarrassing stuff about love—"

"—and Cupcake—"

"—and Sweetpea." Chelsie was grinning again. "Mr. Wilkes is a real killer. He sure keeps things hopping. You're lucky—after the wedding, you'll be related."

I went in the house and brought out two grape Popsicles. I handed hers over with a flourish.

"Last Popsicle of the season," I announced. "School is just days away."

Chels wrinkled her face. "Forget school. Let's promise not to even mention it until Tuesday."

"All right," I said. "I promise."

We shook hands.

"Let's talk about something interesting," Chels said. "What'd you think of *him*?"

"I liked him. Was *that* true, that story? You and Artie really met by accident? You didn't even go over and, you know, turn on the old Bixler charm?"

"It was exactly the way I warned you, Vic. Totally unexpected. You can never predict when love will strike."

My heart jumped. "Love?!" I said. "You're in love? Already?"

"Well, okay, maybe it's not exactly love yet. But close." She paused thoughtfully. "At least there's potential for love."

"Oh." I took another careful lick of the Popsicle, noticing that my fingernails were ugly—short and ragged. My hands needed serious help. The thought was like a dull nagging voice. I wondered why I'd never thought of it before.

"I know what you're thinking, Vic."

"You do?"

"Yeah. You're wondering if Artie's going to wreck our best friendship. Don't worry. Nothing's going to change, just because I have a boyfriend. You and I will always be best friends."

43

That wasn't what I had been thinking about, but it helped . . . even if the idea of Chelsie suddenly having a "boyfriend" hurt a little.

We worked on the Popsicles awhile.

"When you finish that," I said, "will you do me a favor?"

"You're my very, very, very, very finest friend," said Chels regally, bowing to me. "Your wish is my command."

"You're nuts," I said, giving her a slight push. "But could you take a look at the dress Mom and Isadora are making? It's hanging in the closet. Maybe you have some ideas about how to make it less . . . Isadora."

Chelsie smiled a purple grin. "As an acquaintance of mine would say, 'what are friends for?'"

7

"Victoria, what in the world is going on in here?"

It was my mother, coming into the kitchen. She was "dolled up" for work, as Dad would say. Her clothes were pressed and professional, and her hair was shiny and fastened back. She didn't look like someone's mother.

"I'm starting breakfast," I explained, taking another chop at an apple. "I'm making a fruit plate. Fruit plates are supposed to be continental." I didn't exactly know what that meant, but it sounded ritzy. Carefully, I arranged another slice on the platter.

Mom staggered back against the cupboard and put her hand to her heart. "My daughter, ready

45

early, on the first day of school? And helping with breakfast? This is too much."

"Very funny."

"I'll help. Are oranges appropriate on a continental fruit plate?"

"Absolutely."

In the middle of peeling an orange, she stopped. "Isn't that your old red sweater?"

"Yes."

"Don't you usually dazzle your friends with a new outfit the first day of class? Or is my memory failing me?"

It was a complicated answer. "School is tricky," I told her. "On the first day, you want to look nice, but you don't want to look . . . fussy."

"Ohhh," she said.

In no time, we had the table set and the coffee going. It was very cheery.

"Hey," I said, nudging Mom gently, "this is nice. Maybe Dad was right about mornings being worth waking up for."

Mom thought about it. "Naw," she said.

"Howdy," roared Matthew, appearing in the door. "Coming through."

"You get to watch the toaster," I told him. "First, push down the lever. Then stand there and keep an eye on the toast so it doesn't burn."

He didn't squawk or bat an eyelash or anything at the command. He went straight to the counter and snapped down the toast. Then he did a crazy little dance in his plaid school shirt, kicking up his heels.

Mom and I looked at each other.

"What's wrong with you?" my mom asked. "Both of my children are acting strangely this morning."

"I love school," Matthew said, balancing on his heels. "I love going to school."

"How do you know you love it? Today's your first day."

"I just know."

I rolled my eyes. "You'll get over that quick."

"Quickly," Mom said.

I sat down at the table and unscrewed the top of my nail polish.

"What are you doing?" she asked after a second.

"Painting my nails—Ferocious Sunset, to be exact." I knew she wasn't really asking what I was *doing*. When parents ask obvious questions like that, they really mean, "Stop doing that, whatever it is."

"I didn't mean what are you doing. I mean why are you doing that here? Matthew and I are about to keel over from the fumes, and you're going to drip polish onto the tablecloth any second now."

"I'm . . . being . . . very . . . careful," I answered—one slip of the old nail polish brush and you can paint right up to your knuckle.

She made me move so she could slide a whole section of the *Tribune* under my hands. "There. Now I trust you." Carefully she poured coffee into the cups. "Don't forget to jiggle the toaster handle when you think the bread is done, Matthew. That toaster burns every piece of bread it gets its hands on."

"When I was your age, I hated school," I told my brother. "When Dad called upstairs for me to wake up, I'd bury my head under my pillows and pretend I was still asleep. I *loathed* school."

"I don't," he said cheerfully.

Mom sat down in the chair next to me and picked up her mug. "How come you hated school? You were a good student."

"I don't know. Shy, I guess."

"Well, you'd never tell it to look at you now."

School had gotten interesting ever since I had learned about new clothes and guys and friends and things. Now I sort of half loved, half hated it.

"I've matured," I said, swiping the brush down the middle of another fingernail, and passing her a sly grin.

"Can I walk to school with you, Vickie?" my brother asked, out of the blue.

I panicked. I looked at Mom.

Sometimes she is very sensitive. "Aren't you going to walk to school with one of your zillion friends, Matthew?"

"Which friend?"

"How about that little boy who used to always break things? Remember him, Vickie? He fractured his arm playing on the jungle gym, and the day after the cast came off he slipped on some ice and broke a leg. His mother almost had a coronary."

"Yeah," said Matthew. "Everyone called him Peg Leg. The cast was cool; I signed it. He got to stay home and eat ice cream for a week."

"Don't get any ideas, Squirt," I said. I examined my nails. They matched my sweater, and the polish really classed up my kind of grungy hands. A big glob of Ferocious Sunset dripped from the brush I was holding and landed on the newspaper.

"Anyway," said my brother, "I'd rather walk to school with my best sister, Victoria."

What was wrong with him? Didn't he know that walking to school with your little brother is a mistake that no one in Keats Junior High would ever forget?

Dad came into the kitchen singing opera, which he sometimes likes to do in the morning.

"Oh, baby," Mom groaned. "Opera at seven in the morning is like pizza for breakfast."

"What's wrong with it?" he asked, looking hurt. "The kids appreciate it, don't you, guys? When you were a baby, Matthew, you loved my singing."

"He used to throw his bottle at you," Mom reminded him.

"Nonsense. Now, let's see . . . I believe Tosca was his favorite." He paused. "Boy, you guys look great, all of you. What's the occasion?"

He was teasing. I grinned and waved my hand.

"Ah, I remember the day I started first grade," he began grandly. "I— Hey. Do I smell smoke?"

49

Matthew dove for the toaster handle, but it was too late. The bread that popped up was charry black.

"Never mind." Dad put an arm around him. "I like my toast crispy. Drop a couple more slices in the toaster, I'll sing a little opera, and, later, I'll drive you both to school. That way you can dawdle over your breakfast awhile."

We all pulled in our chairs around the table and joined hands.

"Lord," Mom began, "we ask that you would be with each of us today. Protect us, guide us, and show us what you most want us to accomplish today."

"Amen," Dad and I said together.

"Amen," Matthew said, practically shouting.

8

I stepped inside old Keats Junior High, and right away I was part of a crowd moving through the hall. Chelsie, waving to my dad as he pulled away from the building, caught up pretty quick.

"Look at that," she said breathlessly. "Look at all the seventh graders. Did we seem nervous like that when we were in seventh grade?"

I looked at all the unfamiliar faces. Some of the kids were milling around in big groups, trying to look cool. Others seemed sort of lost and lonely. I smiled at a girl heading the opposite way. She just looked startled and hurried past.

"Last year," I reminded her, "we were scared silly. Remember, we couldn't find our homeroom, and you panicked and said you felt like throwing up? And I had to find you the bathroom and then all of a sudden you didn't have to puke after all, and we barely got back to the class before the bell ra—"

"It's all coming back to me," she said grouchily. "No need to bring up all the gruesome details." We walked from the entry into the narrow hallway filled with lockers and other kids.

"Vickie! Chelsie!" a voice rang through the hallway. "Over here!"

A bunch of our friends were standing in a clump, clogging up the hall. We walked faster to join them. Everyone was there—Kristie and Peggy and everyone. We hadn't seen each other much during the summer, on account of my spending the whole vacation at a resort in northern Minnesota, and they all made a big deal about my being back in town.

When the noise died down, Chelsie cleared her throat dramatically. "Notice anything different about me?"

Then everyone was saying, "You got your braces off!"

"Not *that*," she said, patiently. "That's not even close. Is it, Vic?"

I wasn't sure what she was driving at, so I wasn't going to open my mouth. I smiled and shrugged. "If you say so," I said.

"Okay, here goes. I made a big decision over the summer. I became a Christian."

Everyone stared. "Oh," Kristie said, half-heartedly. "Really?"

Chelsie didn't seem to notice. Her face was flushed a happy pink. "Yeah, I accepted Jesus into my life, and it's really great. I have Vic, here, to thank. She's actually the one who—"

"I hate to interrupt," Peggy said suddenly, "but I heard another rumor—that you've been hanging around with some guy."

She didn't even get to finish the sentence before the screams and whistles and questions cut her off. It was wild. Chels just stood in the middle of all the hoopla looking confused, as though she had been interrupted in the middle of a really great story.

They wanted to know every last detail. I got asked all kinds of questions, too, as if I were a witness in a trial. What did he look like? Where did he live? What did he say? What did he wear? I had to give them the whole scoop.

"He's nice," I said to finish up.

It was getting awfully close to bell time, so we started moving down the hall toward our rooms. As we passed open doors, people in the group dropped out and slid inside.

I told Chels I'd walk her to her room, so we headed down the hall. The floor was so clean it reflected our images. Chelsie was tall. I looked like a short blur.

"Everything all right?" I asked. "You got awful quiet back there."

53

"I'm okay," she said.

"We're supposed to be best friends, remember? If something's wrong, you've got to spill it."

"They weren't exactly thrilled about me becoming a Christian, in case you didn't notice. They didn't even care."

"True," I said. There was no use denying it. "I've been a Christian since I was a little kid, so I'm used to it. People don't always want to hear you talk about God. It makes them edgy."

She was walking slower and slower, really dragging her feet. "I just don't get it," she muttered, shaking her head.

"Don't let it bother you," I told her.

We trudged to a stop outside her homeroom.

"But did you see Peg's face? She looked almost disgusted when I mentioned Jesus."

I knew what she was talking about. Sometimes when I mentioned Sunday school or the Bible, I caught friends giving me odd looks, as if I were some sort of crazy person. But I made my voice chipper.

"As good old William Shakespeare would say, 'Much ado about nothing,'" It drives Chelsie wild when I throw around literary quotes like this. "Imagine what John and Peter and Mark and all the disciples went through," I pointed out. "They were *really* persecuted. People hated them."

She looked me hard in the eye. "Yeah, maybe you're onto something. Such as: being a Christian isn't always going to be a piece of cake. I've got to stand up for what I believe and not be embarrassed. Right?"

"Right."

"I sure have to hand it to you, sometimes. You know what you're talking about. Of course, you've had years of experience with these things; you've already been through the hard stuff."

Boy. It sure didn't feel like that to me. Sometimes life seemed *very* hard.

"I'd better get going," I said, shouting above the commotion around us—lockers slamming and tennis shoes squeaking on the shiny floor as kids raced to class. "The bell's going to ring any second."

"Okay, get a move on. You don't want to be late your first day; doesn't make a good impression." She gave my shoulder a light slug. "Vic, I'm glad you're around to give me little pep talks like this. You're one in a million."

"But who wants to be an oddball?" I called back—with only a very small smile—as I turned to retrace my steps to homeroom.

9

At lunch, Chels and I found a bunch of our friends at a table, and they made room for us to sit down. Chelsie watched to see if I was going to pray. I lowered my head and prayed silently. It was strange to think that even in big old Keats cafeteria, God was there. It made me feel good. When I looked up, Chelsie sneaked me a look and a secret smile.

"I'm hoping the food will be better this year," I announced.

"Then you're in for a big disappointment," said Kristie, pushing away her tray.

We tossed most of the food into the garbage. I was careful not to look into the bins; I knew I'd get sick if I ever did.

Chels and I hung around outside for a while.

"You know what's crazy?" I said. "Yesterday it was sunny just like this, and it felt like summer. Today it feels like fall. School changes everything."

"I know what you mean," she said.

I had an idea. "Want to go see Ms. Runebach?" I asked. "We have time."

Ms. Runebach is a teacher who is nice even though she is a teacher. Some teachers are nicer than others, and some don't seem like real people at all. The more teachers I meet, however, the more I realize they're just normal, like kids.

Chels followed me through a side door into the dim hallway. When we poked our heads into Ms. Runebach's classroom, she was there all right, erasing a boardful of notes. She didn't even hear us come in. The notes were about Marjorie Kinnan Rawlings, who wrote a book called *The Yearling*. I know all about it because my English class read it last year. We took turns reading chapters aloud. I got the chapter in which the little deer, Flag, dies. When I got to that part, I almost lost it, right there in class.

"Hi, Ms. Runebach," Chelsie said. "It's us, your two favorite students." We grinned at each other, as if it were a brand-new joke. "Do you know that someone swiped your nameplate? Of all the dirty tricks."

"I wondered when you two would show up," she

said, whirling around. "Actually"—she walked over, jiggling the chalk in her cupped hand—"*I'm* the one responsible for the disappearing nameplate. I took it off the door."

"You probably have a very logical explanation," I said. Besides being nice, Ms. Runebach is extremely intelligent. She wouldn't do anything without a good reason.

"I guess you'll be the first to hear my news. I got married this summer. Now I'm a Runebach-Dahl."

"Dahl as in Mr. Dahl?" Chelsie said. "You married Mr. Dahl, the health teacher? She took a step backward and put her hand to her forehead as if she had a headache. "This is so sudden." Chelsie has acted in some school plays, and sometimes she gets pretty dramatic.

"Congratulations," I said. I stuck my hand out, like my dad does when he's being formal and polite.

"Thanks," she said. "The wedding wasn't all that sudden. We've known each other for a whole year, you know."

"I had him last year," Chels said, "and I'll never forget the day he got up in front of the whole class and announced that he was a bachelor for life, and nothing would make him change his mind."

"Ron said that?" asked Ms. Runebach-Dahl, looking amused.

"They let you teach in the same school?" I said.

"Of course."

"I just figured there'd be some sort of rule."

"As you can see, I'm back, and Ron is just down at the other end of the school. It's very convenient."

"—And romantic," Chels put in.

The door opened, and a kid came in and slid into a seat. Lunch was almost over.

Ms. Runebach-Dahl tossed the chalk into the metal tray and said, "You haven't forgotten about the scholastic essay contest, have you, Vickie? Remember, I nominated you to participate last year?"

"Sure," I said. "I'm already nervous."

"You'll do fine. Over the summer I learned from the contest officials that the theme will be 'open.' That means you can write about anything you want. Quite an opportunity."

Better put on your thinking cap now, Vic," Chels said, nudging me.

"Let me know if you have any flashes of inspiration," said Ms. Runebach-Dahl. She looked at her watch. "Well—"

"Time to shove off," Chels said. "Talk to you soon, Ms. Runebach . . . *Dahl*."

When we got out to the hall, and I was sure Ms. R-D wouldn't hear, I hit the ceiling. "What is this, anyway? Some sort of epidemic?"

"What do you mean?" Chels asked innocently. She was busy dodging people coming toward her in the hall.

"Everyone's falling in love," I said. "You'd think

there was some virus going around."

"Wait a minute. I never said I was in love. I said *maybe* I was. I can't tell yet."

She was terrifically cheerful, humming her little heart out. I knew what she was thinking about. Or, should I say *who*. (Actually, I should probably say *whom*—something Ms. R-D taught me in English.)

"How am I supposed to fall in love," I interrupted, "when I don't know the first thing about it? My *parents* know more about it than I do. Sometimes they carry on and make crazy faces at each other until you can hardly believe they're mature adults."

"It's mysterious, I told you." Chels had a faraway look.

"But I've been a teenager for weeks," I said. "Teenagers are supposed to fall in love."

"Oh, brother." Chelsie rolled her eyes. "Where'd you get that story?"

"From you!" I said. It was outrageous. Here she'd gotten me going on this love business, and now she was going to deny everything. I stewed for a minute without speaking.

There was a decent-looking guy straightening up at the drinking fountain. I flashed him a stunner of a smile, but he just wiped his mouth on his sleeve and walked on.

10

Mr. Wilkes passed the salad and followed it up with Dad's special "house dressing." "How was your first day hitting the old books?" he wanted to know. Everybody at the table was quiet, waiting for an answer.

Matthew's face scrunched up. "Hitting books?" Sometimes he can be awfully literal.

"That means studying," I told him. "It's an expression."

"Oh," he said. He leaned forward until he was practically on top of his helping of lasagne. "In that case," he said, "hitting the books was great. I love it. My teacher's name is Mr. Crawford, and he's kind of bald and has a pet snake named Elmer. He's going to bring Elmer to school tomorrow, and I get to pet him."

That took everyone's breath away for a second. It did sound fairly interesting . . . at least compared to a day spent watching everyone else fall in love.

"Elmer is green and gold," Matthew continued excitedly, through a mouthful of peas. "He has black eyes and a couple of nose holes, and he sleeps on a piece of driftwood."

"Matthew," said Dad, using a stern, fatherly voice, which he only does in emergencies, "can you tell us about some of the other details of your day? You know snakes give me the creeps." He shivered, hunching up his shoulders. "What about other schoollike activities? What about art and math and music—"

Matthew's face lit up like someone had hit a switch. "Music's the best," he said. "We learned about rounds. Want to sing 'Scotland's Burning'? I'll teach you the words. First, I start—"

"Sounds like a real scream," Dad said, smiling. "You can teach us after dinner."

"I brought my harmonica," said Mr. Wilkes, patting his breast pocket.

"All right," said Matthew, looking happy. He picked up his fork and dug into his salad.

"Victoria? Can you top your brother's stories?" asked Isadora. "What was day one of eighth grade like?"

I told them about seeing my old friends and

62

getting issued another locker with a door that sticks. Pretty dull stuff, but they all nodded and looked interested.

Then I delivered the grand finale.

"And," I said, "Ms. Runebach got married. She's Ms. Runebach-Dahl now."

"Imagine having to spell that for people," Mom said, widening her eyes. "Mahoney is bad enough."

Suddenly I had this great idea. It was sneaky, but subtle. I started out carefully. "Of course, Ms. Runebach has always been an individualist. So it figures that her name would be original, too."

"Makes sense to me," Mr. Wilkes said approvingly. "I like a person with originality and spirit." His face sort of melted, and he took hold of Isadora's hand. She got all wilty, too.

I'd have to move fast if I was going to keep the conversation going. *Here goes*, I thought.

"—But she's original in sort of a quiet, understated way." Only the sound of silverware on plates interrupted the silence at the table. Everyone seemed to be concentrating on the food. I repeated the word "understated," cautiously. "For instance, her wedding probably was unique and breathtaking and all, but not too bizarre. You know?"

From across the table, Mom slid me a look. Her eyebrows were sinking low over her eyes.

"—I mean," I continued, "what's a wedding without the bridal march or rice or candlelabras or plain old flowers?"

63

By now Mom's eyes were flashing.

"I couldn't agree with Victoria more." Isadora put down her fork and smiled at me gratefully. "You're wise beyond your years, my dear."

"I am?"

"Oh, my, yes. The point you're making is that everyone needs to have a wedding that suits their personalities, right? The last thing anyone wants is a wedding based on unthinking tradition or flippancy."

"Flip-pansies?" Matthew asked. "Why is everyone using words I can't understand?"

Dad explained what flippancy is, "not taking things seriously enough," which is lucky because I didn't know, either.

"We certainly don't have that trouble," Mr. Wilkes added. "We're taking this wedding very seriously."

Isadora nodded. "Every detail should be mulled over and considered and rethought. Vickie, that reminds me. We need an assistant. I'm sure you have loads of creative ideas. You can help us plan a ceremony that communicates something about *us*. There mustn't be a single stone unturned. No humdrum wedding for us!"

I sank into my seat and stared at my plate.

"A-hem!" said Mom, clearing her throat and giving me a cue. "Will you give me a hand with dessert, Victoria?"

I followed her into the kitchen. As I got out cups

for coffee, she screwed up her face in a very unmotherly expression and whispered, "Serves you right, you little snake in the grass."

Then she handed me a filled mug and pointed me back to the dining room.

"Victoria, are you busy?" After dinner and the dishes were over, Mr. Wilkes poked his head out the back door. "You don't *look* busy, but there could be a good reason for lying on your back in the middle of the lawn."

I didn't move from my lazy position. "Come on out, Mr. Wilkes. I'm just thinking."

He sauntered over, patting his stomach. "One more of your father's meals, and I'll be ready for Weight Watchers. Thinking about what?"

I had been mulling over the wedding. Of course, I couldn't tell him that I was wondering what the guests would think when they saw me in the bumblebee dress. But while I was trying to think of a way to phrase my answer, he said, "I came out to ask you something important."

I sat up. "Shoot."

He looked uncomfortable, and not from the too-large meal. I stood up and walked over to the picnic table. We each took a seat, across the table from each other. I waited patiently for him to start talking.

"I guess I should start at the beginning," he said. "When Izzy proposed to me—"

"Wait a minute. Isadora proposed to *you*?!"

"Yes. Why?"

A man his age should have known that the woman doesn't propose to the man, for crying out loud. Even I knew that.

"Nothing," I said. "Go ahead."

"As I was saying, when your grandmother proposed to me, I realized that one of the things I'd be inheriting was a real, live family. Yours. You remember that I don't have any relatives to speak of?"

I nodded.

"Isadora's bringing a ready-made family to our marriage, and, well, I just love all you guys, right down to that crazy cat of yours."

Anyone who loves Bullrush is a good friend of mine. I felt a surge of warmth for Mr. Wilkes.

"This brings me to the favor I wanted to ask."

We looked at each other.

"Would you mind calling me Grandpa?" He blushed and hurried on. "Just for a while, until you decide if it's okay. I—I wouldn't ask, it's just that I've come to think of you as a granddaughter, and, well, before the wedding would be a good time to try it out. If it doesn't work, we'll just forget about it."

"I could do that," I said, and suddenly I was stuttering, too, as if he had asked me something really embarrassing. "It might take awhile to get the hang of it, but I *already* sort of think of you as

66

my grandfather. A little bit."

"Really?" he asked, looking pleased. "That's a real compliment, Victoria. Thank you." He pushed up from the table, sighing his relief.

"I suppose Isadora wants me to call her Grandma, too," I called as he moved away.

"Isadora?" he said. His face spread in a giant, amused smile. "Oh, no. Grandma Iz? That wouldn't work. That wouldn't work at all." He went into the house, still laughing his deep laugh.

11

Two whole days of freedom! No bells or books or gym coaches.

"It's Saturday, glorious Saturday," I sang at the top of my lungs as I worked my way around the piano, banging into the pedals. Even housework seemed fun, compared to classes. The vacuum cleaner growled raspily, and I gave it a reassuring pat. "Come on, Fido, old boy," I said. "Sic 'em."

It was Dad's idea to name the vacuum Fido. He said it sounded like a disgruntled German Shepherd. I glided under the coffee table and around the couch, running over the electrical cord.

I met Mom in the hallway. "Yoo-hoo!" She was yelling above all the vacuum racket.

"What?" I asked, snapping Fido off and shouting into the suddenly quiet room.

"Phone for you."

I ran to the kitchen. It was Chelsie.

"What was that noise?" she asked. "Your house sounds like a construction site."

"It was only me pushing the Hoover around."

"You were vacuuming?" she said, disbelief in her voice. "You?"

I made sure she could tell I was insulted. "What's so strange about that?"

Chels guffawed. She went on laughing for at least a minute. "You're not exactly homemaker of the year, Vic. I've seen your room, remember?"

"Oh, yeah? What about the clutter in *your* room? You have three junk drawers in your desk."

I'm *afraid* to reorganize. I know where everything is."

I stretched the phone cord across the kitchen and opened the refrigerator, looking for something interesting. Nothing much except jars of pickles and relish and stuff, and a Tupperware container full of sliced carrots. I pulled out a stick.

"What's up?" I asked between chomps.

"Can you come over? I'm conducting an experiment, and I need your help."

"Wait a sec. I'll check." I put down the phone and went out to the living room. Mom was still there, wonderingly wiping a finger over a bookcase.

"You even dusted?" she said. "Your father will be

ecstatic. He hates to dust, and of course, with my allergies, I can't." She put her hands on her hips and grinned wickedly.

"Mom, would you mind if I take some time off from cleaning house?"

"Only for a good reason."

"To visit a friend in need?"

"Chelsie?"

"Right."

"You got it." Then she did a jaunty two-step. "It's hard to get used to, you being so helpful. But I like it. A few minutes ago I was kind of sleepy and dull, but suddenly I'm feeling mighty perky. Think I'll go see what projects I can drum up." Waltzing, she disappeared.

"I'm on my way over," I said over the phone. "Time me." I was out the door in a flash.

Breathless, I leaned on the Bixlers' doorbell. "Eat, drink, and be merry," I said when Chelsie came to her front door, "for in two days we return to school."

"You're telling me," she said, swinging the door open. "Come on in."

She looked pretty spiffy, considering it was just Saturday. I followed her into the kitchen, noticing that her socks matched her shirt. "You dress almost as well as Susie Laplorden," I said.

"Pleeeeze," Chelsie said.

In the kitchen, there were mixing bowls and

70

kitchen utensils all over the counter.

"I'm reading this magazine article about natural facial masks," she told me. "I'm whipping one up at this very moment." She held out a plastic bowl filled with goop. "This is it."

"What's in it?" I asked, leaning over and looking at the lumpy mixture.

"Uncooked oatmeal. Wheat germ. Mashed cucumber. Egg white."

"Ick."

"Yeah. But wait till you see what it does for skin."

She made me help smear it on her face. It was sticky and cold. She got me laughing, and I had to stand there for a while with my one hand stuck in the bowl and the other holding onto the counter so I wouldn't fall on the floor.

"Hurry!" she shouted, trying to catch her breath. "This stuff's starting to dry!"

Finally we got her whole face covered. We left patches around just her eyes and her mouth.

"Now what?" I said, pulling up a stool at the kitchen counter.

She looked at her watch. "We wait twenty minutes."

I flipped through the *TV Guide*. "Want to watch a bad movie? Here's one: *Slimy Monsters of the Deep*."

Chelsie made an exaggerated yawn. Then she

slapped her hand against her hip. "Let's call Artie."

"Huh?" I said, like I was a moron or something.

"Yeah, why can't we call him and say we'll meet him at the swimming pool in an hour?"

The idea of wearing a bathing suit to a public pool is awful enough, let alone wearing it with some guy around. But Chelsie was already starting to weasle me into it. Actually, it did sort of sound fun.

"Come on, Vic. It's no big deal. Do me this one favor."

"Don't you guys want to be alone?" It was the kind of cornball line I probably picked up from TV or something.

Chels burst out laughing. "Of course not. My parents would kill me if I went out alone with Artie. I'm too young to date—at least, that's what Mom tells me." She put her elbows on the counter and leaned toward me, until her wheat-germ-oatmeal-egg-white mask was right in my face. "What's your answer, small friend?"

"Okay, okay," I said. She always gets to me when she makes me laugh.

I about had a fit watching her talk to Artie on the phone. The mask kept dripping onto the floor. But Chelsie kept her cool, I noticed. She didn't get all stupid and giggly.

"All set," she told me, hanging up. "Public swimming pool, one hour sharp. I knew that would appeal to him. He's pretty sports minded."

We settled down on the carpeting, on our sides,

with our heads propped up against our elbows. We do some of our best thinking in this position; I don't know why. I think it might improve our circulation.

"You know what happened?" Chelsie said. She got very serious. I knew enough not to interrupt her when she was serious. "The other day in class some of the kids started telling jokes, except they weren't funny. They were crummy. You know what I mean. At first I just ignored them. Then this guy jabs me and says, 'Hey, what's wrong with you? You're not one of those straight religious types, are you?'"

"What did you say?"

"I said 'No, I'm not one of those religious types.' It was terrible. For the first time, I knew how Peter felt. You know, when people asked him if he was associated with Jesus, and he lied and said he wasn't. I *wanted* to say, 'Yeah, I'm a Christian,' I really did. But I was afraid. I didn't know what would happen."

"I know," I said.

Her mouth turned down. She looked like one of those crazy theatrical masks. "I knew what was *right*," she said, "and I didn't do it. I feel crummy."

"That's the great thing about God," I said. "He forgives you no matter what."

"What if the same thing happens again?"

"Ask Him to get you ready ahead of time. Pray that He'll give you the guts to stand up for what you believe in."

Chelsie considered this. "I can try, I guess. I'm still getting used to all this, you know, realizing that God's always there and everything. I've been handling things on my own for years."

"Hey," I said. "Isn't it time yet to wash off that junk?"

"Yeah. Come with me."

We trooped over to the sink, and Chels splashed water around and mopped her face up with a dish towel.

"How's it look?" she asked.

I got up close, close enough to see pores. "Okay, I guess."

I look different, don't I?"

"Nope. Not really." I had to be honest.

Her face fell practically to her socks. "Great," she said. "Vic, I don't think this beauty business is everything it's cracked up to be. Who says you have to have perfect skin in the first place?"

I started to say, "Not *me*." I happen to think all that fluffy girl stuff is overrated (even though I have been known to wear eye shadow now and then). But she looked so disappointed, I tried to cheer her up instead. "I don't know what you're worried about. Your skin is already perfect."

But she didn't seem to hear me. When she gets rolling, there's no putting the brakes on.

"And who said girls have to be interested in all this junk, anyway?" She started rinsing our mixing bowls and stuffing eggshells down the garbage disposal. "My mom gets into all of that, you know, the whole beauty routine. But why should I have to worry about being a raving beauty? There are more important things in life."

I could have said something like, "If that's true, how come you look so disappointed?" but I didn't. I flicked some dried oatmeal off her arm. "Let's go swimming," I said softly instead.

12

The news reached me before I made it down the hall to my Sunday school classroom: "New kid, new kid." Everyone was whispering. It's always big news when there's someone new in class.

He was already sitting at the table, right next to Sharon Hilliard.

"Hi," she said to me, which was really something because Sharon is the shiest person, practically, in the whole world. I said "Hi" back, with a smile, and "Did you read the lesson?" I always try extra hard to be nice to Sharon, because I know what it's like to be sort of scared.

The new kid didn't say anything.

Mr. Bjork came in and got everyone calmed

down. "Sharon," he said, "why don't you introduce your friend?"

Sharon went purple. Then she said, "Um, this is Skip, and he's my cousin. He's trying my church out today. He doesn't know if he'll be back or anything."

There were a couple of snickers. "Skip your real name?" someone asked.

Skip didn't say yes or no. He just sat there, looking kind of far-off and dreamy, like he might as well have been sitting on a grassy hill somewhere. Suddenly he pushed his longish blond hair out of his eyes and looked up, right at me. There was a sudden catch in my breath. Or maybe it was in my stomach. I'm not sure which. *This is it*, I thought. *Finally I'm in love.*

While Mom, Dad, and Matthew were upstairs changing out of their church clothes, I dialed Chelsie's number.

She answered on the first ring.

"Hello?"

"It's me. Why weren't you at church?"

"I'm sick." She sniffed. "It was so dumb to walk home from the pool yesterday with wet hair. My mom is furious. She keeps coming upstairs to give me dirty looks and make me drink gallons of orange juice."

"You sound awful."

"Thanks." She sniffed again.

77

I lowered my voice significantly. "I have big news."

"What?"

"*It* finally happened."

"It? What's *it*?"

"Love . . . I think."

"At church? You fell in love at church?"

"There was a new kid in Sunday school. Sharon Hilliard's cousin. His name's Skip Hilliard."

"Skip Hilliard. Hmmm. What happened?"

"Well," I said. "Not much, exactly. He did kind of look at me."

"And I missed it. I could just kill myself. Tell me, did your eyelids twitch? My eyelids twitched when I first saw Artie. Actually it was just one eyelid. Maybe it was a muscle spasm or something."

"My eyelids didn't do a thing. But my stomach kind of bunched up."

"That's it!" she shouted and then had to stop talking while she had a coughing fit.

"The silence at this table is killing me." Dad looked around with big eyes. "Is there something going on here that I don't know about?"

"I'm not in on it," said Mom.

Sunday dinners are a big tradition at our house. When Dad has a day off from the restaurant, we usually sit around hashing stuff over. We've had some pretty interesting conversations over baked sweet potatoes, broccoli with toasted almonds, and

78

whole wheat rolls with real butter.

I spoke up. "If you want to know the truth, I was thinking about love."

"Vickie's in love! Vickie's in love!" Matthew screeched.

"Now that's an interesting subject." Mom ladled spinach fettucini noodles onto my plate. "Ask us anything; we're experts. Aren't we, Terry?"

My dad smiled and fluttered his eyelashes. Maybe that was the twitching Chels had been talking about. I made a mental note to watch myself closely for fluttering eyelids.

"Chelsie's in love with this guy," I told them. "She even caught cold yesterday because she wouldn't dry her hair after swimming. She had to walk home with wet hair because she thought Artie'd get bored of waiting and leave."

"Love makes people do crazy things," Mom put in. "Remember the time Matthew took a whole package of ice-cream sandwiches over to his girl friend? By the time he made it to her house, there was vanilla ice cream everywhere. It dripped out of the box the whole way. The neighbors thought it was hilarious. What was that little girl's name again?"

"Heidi Little," I supplied. "She was cute."

Matthew wrinkled up his face. "Bleckkkk," he said, crossing his eyes.

"You used to like her," I pointed out.

"No way. I hate girls. I'm in first grade now."

Mom put down her fork ominously. Parents don't like you to say you hate people, even if you're only exaggerating.

Matthew backed down. "Okay, maybe I don't hate her. But I don't *like* girls, anyway."

Dad helped himself to more fish. "Give yourself a couple years. It's amazing how things change." He gave me one of his winks and a lopsided grin. "Isn't that right, Victoria?"

Probably I was blushing. Even though they didn't know about Skip, it was embarrassing to be put on the spot. I moved food around on my plate.

Usually acting uninterested can get me off the hook, but even when I looked back up, Dad was still giving me the eye, one brow cocked knowingly. My parents get sharper all the time.

Finally Dad picked up his fork and speared some fettucini. "Speaking of love, have you heard the latest about the Wilkes-Shippley wedding? Harold is driving to Wisconsin to buy a carload of fresh apples so he can concoct his famous homemade applesauce to serve at the reception."

"Don't most people serve cake?" I asked.

"Sure," said Mom, "but applesauce is a lot more original than a fattening old white cake covered with frosting."

"I have a hunch that applesauce is only the beginning. This is going to be one wild wedding," Dad said.

He could say that again.

13

Isadora rapped her wedding-planning notebook with a pen. "You've got to pay attention, Vickie," she said, shaking her head. "You're supposed to be brainstorming, not staring into space like a zombie."

I pulled my eyes away from the high-in-the-sky view from Isadora's apartment window. "I'm thinking," I said.

"You're daydreaming," she said knowingly. "I know daydreaming when I see it." She looked me over closely. "What is it? Boy problems?"

Good grief. Was it that obvious? I wiped all the expression right off my face.

"Do you want to get it off your chest?" she asked,

leaning forward and peering closely at me.

I recrossed my legs. Talking about my chest makes me very nervous. "No, thanks, I'm ready to get back to the wedding now."

"All right." Isadora bit the end of her pencil. "As I was saying, we need to find a place to have the wedding."

"A church," I said. "Most people have weddings in a church."

"Yes, we could do that," she said, printing "church" on the paper. "Of course, that's fairly traditional, isn't it? We needn't close off our options. Think. Where else would be interesting? What about a park? We could have a lovely service in a park. Of course, it might be a little chilly in Minnesota that time of year. Do you think the guests would mind standing up to their knees in snow?" She cackled. "No, we'll have to come up with something else."

"How about the zoo?" I said, matching her hysterical mood and trying to be funny.

"Hmm," said Isadora, musing. "The zoo. that's an idea."

My jaw dropped down to my knees. "Isadora," I said, "I was just kidding. It was a joke."

"I hear Como Zoo has a new reptile house . . . ."

"*Isadora!*"

"Okay, okay," she said. "But I'm going to put it down anyway—just in case we run out of ideas." She scratched "Como Zoo" onto the list.

We both jumped at a forceful knock that shook the door on its hinges—not to mention the foundation of the building. Isadora strode across the room and swung open the door.

"Harold! I'm glad you're here!"

They kissed.

I have always wondered if older couples kiss like younger couples. It looked the same. They even made noise.

Isadora took him by the hand and drew him inside. "Victoria and I are planning the wedding. Make yourself at home. You can give us your two cents worth."

"Hi, Victoria," he said, almost shyly.

"Hi," I said back. We hadn't seen each other since the day he asked me to call him Grandpa. I'd been practicing, but it still felt funny. I hoped I could get through the conversation without having to refer to him.

Mr. Wilkes sat back in the chair and groaned. Some older types do that when they sit down—back problems or something. He rubbed his hands as if he were sitting in front of a roaring bonfire. "I have truckloads of ideas," he said. "Barn loads. Trainloads."

"Let's talk about music, then. What would make an interesting wedding march?"

Before anyone could speak, I put in, "My cousin had a string quartet at his wedding. It was great. Very romantic and classy. They had the prelude

83

music taped, and sometimes when they have company for dinner, they slap it into the cassette player and pretend it's just regular dinner music. Only the two of them know what it's really from."

"Oh, I like that," Isadora said, writing on the paper. "String quartet."

"And I have a friend at the senior citizens' home who plays the accordion," piped up Mr. Wilkes. "He belts out those polkas like nobody's business. Oom-pah-pah, oom-pah-pah. I can just see it—there's the string quartet fiddling away, and old Ed's marching up the aisles playing 'Lady of Spain'!" He practically doubled over and slapped his knee.

Isadora and Mr. Wilkes got a good chuckle out of that one, but I wasn't laughing. I was picturing myself cavorting behind old Ed in the yellow bumblebee dress.

14

Chelsie flicked my arm. "Are you nervous? You're acting nervous."

I turned to her. In the puddle of light cast by the streetlight in the church parking lot, her face was shadowy and slightly scary. "I'm not nervous."

"You've been pushing your hair behind your ears for the last fifteen minutes, which you only do when you're keyed up."

"Okay, maybe I *am* a little jittery."

We huddled together, surrounded by the other youth group kids. I crossed my arms, trying not to look cold, waiting for the annual fall scavenger hunt to begin. The kids at the far end of the lot were just silhouettes in the dark. Even from where I was standing I could recognize Skip. And *that* was the explanation for my nervousness. He was standing with a bunch a kids and his cousin, grinding his tennis shoes into the gravel.

"Loosen up," Chelsie said, giving me the elbow. "It'll be fun."

Mr. Bjork called for attention. "I'm dividing you into groups of four. Gather together for the reading of the groups!"

"Skip's gonna be in our group," Chelsie whispered to me, as he started calling out names. "I sort of requested it."

"You what?!" I didn't know whether I was furious with her or pleased.

"Well, I had to do something. You've been avoiding this guy for weeks. If I have to sit another Sunday watching you ignore old Skip, I'll scream."

"You can't rush into stuff like this!" I protested.

"I can."

Maybe Mr. Bjork already had the groups divided, or maybe he wouldn't pay any attention to Chelsie's suggestion—

"Chelsie Bixler!" Mr. Bjork called. "Vickie Mahoney! Sharon Hilliard! Skip Hilliard!"

Chels didn't say anything or even nudge me. We both stared straight ahead like statues.

Mr. Bjork reviewed the general scavenger hunt rules and handed out lists. We had to go from house-to-house and ask if they had the items.

"Don't forget," added Mr. Bjork. "Only houses

with lights on. And pay attention to your maps. No one goes outside the established neighborhood boundaries. Be sure to explain where you're from and what you're doing. Be polite: remember, you'll be representing the church. Okay, go ahead. Have fun."

Chelsie grabbed my arm and started dragging me toward our other group members.

The darkness at the end of the parking lot was eerie.

"Hi, Vickie," Sharon said, as we walked out of reach of the lot lights.

"Hi, Sharon. Hi, Skip." I smiled at Sharon, like I do every Sunday, and then looked over at him. He was cute, very cute, and he was looking back at me. I didn't feel so cold anymore.

"Howdy," he said.

"At last," I heard Chelsie mutter. Then, before I could glare at her, she said, "Let's get going. We've gotta win. Give me the list."

She had to hold the sheet close to make it out:

raw eggs!
old bottle nail polish
fortune cookie
3 mothballs
pizza carton
toilet paper, pink—2 rolls
knotted rope
false eyelash
wooden spool

Once we got rolling, it was fun. The first couple houses didn't have anything. We all said "Thank you" very politely and moved on. After a little while, though, we started loosening up. We weren't having much luck. When about the fifth person said they didn't have any of the stuff, Sharon blurted out, "Oh, drat, drat!" I had to chomp down on my lip to keep from laughing, it sounded so funny.

Skip seemed really pretty friendly. "It's my turn, guys!" he announced at one house. He marched right up the steps and rattled off the spiel about being from the church and stuff.

The lady at the door looked a little confused. "But I don't have any of those things," she said.

"Oh," said Skip. "That's okay. We'll just—"

"But wait a second," she said, starting to turn and go back inside. "I have *other* things you could have. I have a whole *mess* of painted cotton balls."

We looked at each other with widening eyes. Skip called out, "Um, thanks, ma'am, but, um, no thanks," and we took off. We dashed at about 100 mph to the next house, laughing our heads off.

"Oh, my stomach," said Chels, doubling over. "It hurts!"

"Don't make me laugh!" cried Skip, laughing as if he'd never stop.

"We've gotta get control of ourselves," Sharon gasped. "We have to keep moving or we'll never get all this stuff!"

Slowly we shaped up and started moving up the sidewalk to another front door. I rang the doorbell.

A man with a thin, unsmiling face and not much hair answered, snapping on the light abruptly.

"What is it?" he said, not opening the screen.

Sharon began telling him about the youth group. Her words came out choppy because she had been running. This nearly made us break up all over again.

"Do you have any of the things on this list?" Sharon asked him. "So far we only have the eggs and the toilet paper, so we still need—"

"Get out of here, you crazy kids," snapped the man. "I don't have time for this nonsense."

Everyone just stared at him. We were stunned senseless.

"Get off of my property, and stay away from here, or I'll—I'll call the police." We were all still standing there motionlessly. Finally he barked out, "Now!" and shut the door in our faces, putting out the porch light. We could hear his footsteps fade away inside the house.

In the dark, Sharon's eyes were watery. "Let's get out of here," she said.

We walked silently back down the sidewalk.

"I can't believe it," Chelsie said. She sounded like she had all the laughter whipped right out of her. She was very quiet, looking at her feet.

Suddenly Sharon was crying. "Why did he have to yell at us?" I always knew she was sensitive, so I guess I shouldn't have been surprised. It was just very uncomfortable, because I didn't know her well enough to know what to say. "It's okay," was all I could think of, which made her sob harder.

"That old grouch," Skip said, stopping on the curb. "What was his problem?"

Nobody had an answer.

"Okay," he said, "here's what we have to do." We all looked at him.

"It's a revenge plan," he said.

"What is it?" Chells asked hesitantly.

"It's so brilliant, it's beautiful," he said. "First we t.p. the place. Every last centimeter. The shrubs, the house, the mailbox, everything. Then we hide in the bushes. I ring the doorbell. When he comes to the door, pow! We pelt the screen with eggs."

We all stood looking at him. It did sound like a good idea. My anger was still fresh. A fall breeze came up. It scuttled some scratchy leaves on the sidewalk. I shivered and took a breath.

"I don't want to do it."

Skip turned to me. He wasn't smiling. "Why not?"

"It'd be a crummy thing to do," I said. "I can't do it."

"What's wrong with you?" Skip demanded. The breeze blew his hair wildly. Even in the dark I could tell that he was scowling. "Does it say in the Bible that you can't t.p. someone's house?"

My mind had gone blank. "It just doesn't seem

90

right," I said. "I don't want to do it."

The silence was huge. Chelsie looked at her feet. Sharon sniffed. She shrugged. "Whatever," she said.

"Oh, forget it," Skip said, shoving his hands into his jacket pockets angrily. "Forget I ever brought it up. Let's get on with this stupid scavenger hunt. Maybe we can still win."

I moved fast, leading the way. My heart was pumping energy into my legs and feet, arms and hands. But Skip edged by me on the sidewalk, taking long strides.

"You sure are an odd one," he said as he passed. He laughed, but it was not a nice sort of laugh.

15

Chels and I were halfway to school. We hadn't
said much to each other besides "Hi ya," which is
unusual for us. I could feel her giving me side
glances, but I didn't feel much like talking. She was
walking faster and faster. I knew something was
going to blow any minute—that's how well I know
Chelsie.

"Well, *que sera, sera,*" she burst out. She is big
on exotic phrases like this. "You're not depressed
about old Skip the Drip, are you? Because, to tell
the truth, I wasn't all that impressed with him, after
the first blazing impression wore off."

"I'm not depressed," I said.

"You could have fooled me," she said. "Your chin

is dragging on the pavement. You have a big, gloomy storm cloud right over your head."

"Okay," I said. "You're right. I'm depressed. Do we have to talk about it?"

"Yes, we do. It's up to concerned friends like me to wring the truth out of friends like you. You'll feel better after you talk it out with your best bosom friend. It'll be therapeutic."

"What's to talk about? That was the shortest romance on record. Come to think of it, it wasn't much of a romance."

The biting fall wind had made Chelsie's cheeks bright pink. She turned to me. "In my humble opinion, Skip isn't half good enough for you."

"He's cute."

"True. And if he ever happens to shape up, maybe—just maybe—you'll be available. Providing you haven't already found someone really eligible."

"Yeah," I said, letting out a short laugh. "Maybe a miracle will occur."

She slapped my back. "Oh, buck up, you old sourpuss."

We passed Artie's house in silence. I hadn't seen Artie in ages, and it didn't look like Chels wanted to talk about him, either. Her jaw was tight, as if she were biting on peanut brittle.

A block past, Chels started to laugh.

"I was just thinking of what you said the other night. You really showed old Skip a thing or two. You really stuck to your guns."

"Why didn't you say so then?" I put in. "I could have used the support."

That made her stop laughing. "You're right," she admitted. "I *should* have stuck up for you. You did the right thing, and the least I could have done is stood by you. I'm some lousy friend, huh?"

"Oh, you're okay," I said.

"You forgive me?"

"Yeah, I forgive you. Yes."

Chelsie kicked some leaves. Her feet disappeared under the carpet of elm leaves. "I have realized something earth shattering. You want to hear it?"

"Sure. Shoot."

"If you want to be a Christian, you should be willing to be different. Even if there's no one to stand with you."

"That's true."

"And who do you think showed me that?"

I shrugged.

"You did, silly. You're my idea of a Christian who's willing to go out on a limb."

A fuzzy glow started working its way through my shoulders. It snaked down my spine and into my elbows and my fingers, and down to my heels.

"Really?" I asked, but I already knew she meant it. Chels doesn't say stuff unless she means it. "Anyway," I pointed out, "that doesn't help about Skip. I feel lousy and I still don't know anything about love. Maybe I'll never know."

"Yeah, I know what you mean. I've begun to wonder about Artie, too. He's sort of juvenile sometimes. A couple of nights ago he called and talked all about this sports stuff, all about *him*, and I was so bored I could have screamed. I didn't scream—which would probably have broken his eardrum—but I wanted to."

Suddenly I realized there were rustly footsteps behind us. I turned. It was our old pal, Peggy. She grinned and hurried to catch up, her blonde hair bouncing on her shoulders.

"I was going to follow y'all all the way to school like this," she said. "But you caught me."

We walked three across.

"Anything new?" she wanted to know.

"Oh, nothing much," said Chelsie airily. "Except we've both just had our first bitter experience with love."

Peggy went wild. Curiosity was written all over her face. She supposedly had a boyfriend over the summer, but I think it was more talk than anything else.

"We're jaded, all right," Chelsie continued. "We'll probably never trust another guy as long as we live."

I had a great idea then. I said, "When we're twenty-one, Chels, let's find a great apartment somewhere and buy white wicker furniture and hang pots and pans from the ceiling and park our bikes in the living room. We could have a whole houseful of cats and never worry about falling in love or anything."

"Count me in," said Chels. "That's a great idea. Let's forget about our love lives. Things would sure be less complicated."

"Besides," I said, suddenly getting this terrible thought. "I won't have time for any more of this love business. My next project is helping to keep Isadora and Mr. Wilkes—I mean, Grandpa—from turning their wedding into a circus. And believe you me, that will be a full-time job."

16

Beep, beep, beep. The beeper that signaled afternoon announcements didn't quiet down the classroom. The principal cleared his throat over the intercom and started bumbling through the announcements again. I don't think he would ever make a good disc jockey, no matter how hard he tried.

After an announcement about all lost gym socks getting tossed after school today if we didn't get into the office to claim them, he paused and said, "And now I'd like to turn the mike over to an old friend of the student body. She has a very special message."

"Hello, friends," said a woman's voice. It was a

nice, warm voice that sounded familiar. "This is Isadora Shippley, and I do have an important message. I'm getting married, and I want you all to come to the ceremony."

"Since I can't possibly get invitations to all of you, I'm letting you know about my plans through this little radio address. Those of you who worked on the play production sets with me last year, and even those of you whom I've never met, please feel free to show up at my wedding on November 29. That's the weekend after Thanksgiving, and there's no excuse for you not to come. Just give me a little advance warning, an RSVP, a call, something, so we can make plans."

The other kids in class were ogling me, and I didn't blame them. I keep thinking I'm used to Isadora, and then she surprises me again. The principal signed off, the bell rang, and we filed into the hall.

"Yoo-hoo!" A shrill voice came down the hall after me. It was Isadora, coming at a gallop. Her hair was flying out behind her, and she was grinning to beat the band. "You haven't forgotten that we're getting together this afternoon, have you? To help with wedding plans?"

How could I possibly forget, I wondered, with her announcing her wedding to the whole student body over the intercom?

She fell into step beside me, and I led the way to my locker. Every couple of feet, someone would call out, "Hi, Iz!" It seemed that everyone was her friend since her debut as set designer for the play last year.

Isadora shouted across the hallway to the kids who greeted her. She's not exactly the shy type.

Outside it was raining buckets. We hunched together under her umbrella.

"Let's take a bus," she suggested, "instead of trying to make it to my apartment on foot. I don't feel like traipsing all over the city in a downpour; I'm too tired from all the finagling with musicians and park officials. But I'll tell you that story later."

The bus showed up. We found seats in front and back of each other.

"I hope my little intercom message didn't embarrass you," Isadora said, twisting around to get a look at me. "It was the best way I could think of to invite everyone to the wedding. Harold was just wild about the idea, and I had to rush right over and do it."

"It was okay," I said. "But I'll warn you ahead, you better order more food for the reception. When you offer free food at Keats, the whole student body will probably turn out."

"The more the merrier," Isadora said cheerfully. "Thanks for stopping over tonight." She patted my hand. "I can use your help."

I looked out at the rainy world. The gutters were rushing with rivers of rain, and the bus dashed through big puddles, spraying pedestrians.

I was almost afraid to ask. "What plans have you made so far?"

"Okay," she said, getting businesslike. "One thing is shoes. Now, I know this doesn't sound romantic, but I want to wear tennis shoes to the wedding."

I rolled my eyes clear up into my head. I have heard stories of kids who have had their eyes get stuck this way, but in this case, I couldn't help it.

"Tennis shoes at a wedding?" I said.

"They're comfortable," she said. "I'll be on my feet all day."

"But they'd look crazy!" I said.

"I'm open to better ideas."

I didn't have time to answer, because we were at her stop. We climbed out onto the sidewalk.

"How about ballet slippers?" I shouted, as the bus roared away. *"They're* comfortable."

She considered. "That seems reasonable. Okay. Forget the tennis shoes; I'll go with the slippers. Now. What about flowers?"

"Something simple and sophisticated. How about long-stemmed white roses? They're traditional."

"Cut flowers?" Isadora shouted, right there on the street. A man trying to fit his key into the lock of his car looked up curiously. "You want me to *cut* flowers for the wedding?"

"What's wrong with that?" I said.

"What's wrong? What's wrong? I'll tell you. I will not kill living things, that's what's wrong."

We were scurrying for her building, and I decided to let her cool down before I went on with the conversation. That would be safest. She put her key in the lock and let us into the building. Dripping, we waited for the elevator. When the doors opened, we stepped inside. A woman in multicolored curlers moved to the back.

"What's wrong with cutting flowers?" I asked.

"I just won't do it," she said, crossing her arms. "I was thinking of potted flowers instead."

"Potted flowers? You mean on the platform?" I asked.

"No, I mean in our bouquets. You and me."

"We're going to carry potted plants?" I asked. "You mean like African violets or geraniums or something?"

"Precisely. Afterwards, we can all troop outside and plant them. That would be a positive ecological statement, I think."

"That would be weird, that's what I think." It had been bottled up so long, there was no stopping the explosion, and I let her have it. I told her the whole plan was pretty crazy.

"Victoria!" she said, her eyes wide. "I'm surprised at you."

Instantly I felt guilty. The woman behind me in the elevator didn't say anything, but in the reflective elevator mirror I could see that she was looking at me with a parently expression of disapproval.

17

"Maybe you're right," Isadora was saying, as we tramped down the hall to her apartment. "Maybe I should go traditional and be done with it."

Of course now I was apologizing all over the place and kicking myself for blowing up. *Why do I do that, Lord?*

"It's okay," Isadora kept saying. "No harm done." She knocked hard on the door. We waited.

"That's odd," she said. "Harold said he'd meet us here. He planned to be back from his apple hunting by two o'clock. The rain must have slowed him down." She knocked hard again.

"Well, let's get something done," she said, finding her keys and unlocking the door. "Harold can join us when he gets in."

Isadora's apartment was dark and warm. She switched on a light, and the place lit up cozily.

After we had dried out our hair with clean towels and put the teakettle on, Isadora pulled up a chair and picked up her pen. "Ready? One thing we've been thinking about is renting an open-air carriage after the ceremony. I know most folk just decorate a car with the old aerosol-whipping-cream-and-tin-can routine, but this was Harold's idea. I think it's quaint, the idea of riding through the streets in a horse-drawn carriage. It's apt to be a bit nippy, but don't you think it sounds romantic?"

It did, it really did. (Though what did I know about romance, for pete's sake?) "Put it down," I said.

Lightning cracked bright across the sky. We drank our tea and tried to imagine what people would say when they saw the bride and groom whisking by in a carriage. I could just picture it—Mr. Wilkes waving to everyone, like the mayor of Minneapolis, and Isadora scattering apple seeds or lawn fertilizer or something. The idea got me hysterical, and I choked on my tea.

Next we split up phone calls to make. She wanted some of the kids from school to help paint a backdrop, and she wanted Dad's restaurant to cater the reception (everything but Mr. Wilkes's world-famous applesauce).

"You better keep it quiet about the catering," I

said. "If Mom hears about cookies and brownies, she'll want us to take all the sugar out and add sunflowers and raisins instead."

Isadora grimaced. "Mum's the word."

The light over the table suddenly blinked out.

"This is some storm." Iz thunked around in the kitchen and found a candle; then struck a match. The flame shook, but she got the candle lit. We looked out over the street, and it was desolate and wet.

Isadora tried Mr. Wilkes's number again.

"This makes me nervous," she said in a strange, strained voice. "Harold is never late."

She went over to the clock and turned the winding key until the springs were probably ready to explode, and then she walked to the other end of the room and adjusted a ceramic vase. It was the same vase I had knocked into a few weeks ago when I was clowning around with Matthew. It had landed on the floor and part of the rim had snapped right off. But Isadora had just said, "Never mind," and fixed it with Krazy Glue. Now she pushed it a fraction to the left and then back to the right. She kept pacing.

"I'd forgotten about this," she said. "It's the part of love you never hear about. The responsibility. The worry." She paused for a moment. "There's more to love than flash-in-the-pan romance. You probably think that's taking the fun out of love. But you'll understand when you're older."

That made me think of Skip the Drip again, and my heart felt this funny little pinching grip.

"What?" asked Isadora, stopping and looking at me. "Why did you make that face?"

"Because," I said, "I have decided love is for the birds."

"Really?" Isadora asked, looking interested. "Why?"

I didn't really feel like opening *that* depressing can of worms. "I'm never going to fall in love," I said. "Not if I can help it."

"Aw." She waved her hand at me impatiently. "How do you know? Maybe you won't, and maybe you will. Perhaps you'll even decide someday to get married."

"I hope not," I said. "Chels would be furious—after we rented that apartment and everything."

Isadora stopped pacing. "What apartment?"

"The one with the white wicker furniture and all the cats."

"Oh." She started pacing again.

I helped myself to a cookie or two. "How did you know Mr. Wilkes was the one?" I asked, my mouth full. This is one of the benefits of spending time with someone you know pretty well. You don't always have to be on your best behavior.

That question stumped her for a second. She had to come and sit down and put her hand under her chin and think about it. "I'll tell you," she said. "It was an amazing thing."

I settled in for the story.

"Now, you know I wasn't looking for anyone, Victoria. You know I was perfectly content to live alone, painting and grabbing life by the horns."

"I know," I said.

"And I didn't need anyone to look after me, or keep me company. I survived many a year all on my own, with God's help—just me and my work."

"I know," I said.

"—And then you introduced me to Harold. Nice man, but a little strange. Spent the livelong day perfecting crafts for that senior citizens' group."

"Right," I said.

"But one night I invited him over for coffee, and we got to chatting."

"What about? Stuff you have in common?" Certain magazines I have read say you should always ask someone of the opposite sex about things they are interested in. Stuff I never got the chance to ask Skip.

Isadora shook her head until the red-tipped hair bobbed. "We tried, but it seemed we had nothing in common. Nothing. It was very nearly funny. I would say, 'I love a crisp winter day,' and he would look gruff and reply, 'Crisp winter days depress me!' We contradicted everything the other said." Her voice dropped confidentially. "By the time we had done this five or six times, Harold was truly irritated. He was getting a little red in the face— which he will deny, of course, but it's true.

"And then we happened to hit on the subject of our past lives, and he began telling me the story of his wife. She passed away years ago, you know, but he described her as if it had been yesterday. He told how he visited her every day after she got sick with cancer. He would walk to the bus stop—they had no car, you see—and wait for a #29. And when it arrived, he rode to the hospital, praying the whole way.

"At the hospital he took the elevator to the cancer floor. There he took hold of Edith's hand. She was in a lot of pain, and when neither one of them could stand it any longer, he would begin reading aloud. The newspaper first. Then funny stories and poems and articles. Once he acted out a Christmas drama called, 'Rudolph's Big Adventure,' playing all the parts. The nurses scurried by, giving him very odd looks."

I listened without moving a centimeter; my chest felt as if it had been wound as tight as the clock.

"When it got late and the lights were turned off, Harold would finish the evening by reciting a psalm. He said it got him through the rattling cold bus ride home in the dark. And finally, one afternoon in February, Edith died. He was with her, and she just passed away.

"When Harold got to the end of his story, there were tears in both our eyes. And he said, 'Well, Isadora, now we have something in common. We have a memory together.' And I thought, 'Now here's an exceptional person.' "

Our tea was getting cold. Isadora went on in a low and tender voice.

"Do you know why he runs himself ragged to teach those senior citizens' classes? Because he was so lonely himself during that period in his life. 'If only someone had been around that winter,' he says. So he goes over to the center to see if he can be a friend to any of the people there."

She was going about sixty miles an hour. I couldn't have stopped her if I'd wanted to.

"—Of course, I haven't even *mentioned* the fact that Harold doesn't say 'boo' about all my odd little habits. He accepts me exactly as I am." Her face looked older, tired. "I know I'm not your typical grandmother, Victoria. I don't dress right or do things the safe, conventional way. For your sake, I sometimes wish I could be more like regular folk . . . ."

I got up, and my arms went around her scrawny shoulders, hugging hard. "You're perfect, Isadora," I said, just as the door rattled with a firm, familiar knock.

"Honey, you're back," Isadora said, throwing herself into Mr. Wilkes's arms. He stood in the doorway looking pleased and puzzled.

"Miss me?" he asked.

"Not only did we miss you," I said, because Isadora was too busy being mushy and all, "but we were worried sick. You're late!"

"I know. The roads were terrible; I couldn't even pull off to call. Halfway there I almost turned around and came back. Then I had a thought: What would the wedding be without applesauce? So I drove on. I had no idea roads would be so treacherous on the way home." Gently he pulled out of Isadora's grasp and gathered up great bulging sacks. "Know what's in here? Crisp tart apples. Jonathans and Milsaps and Macintosh. Not your average wimpy specimens. These are hearty. They're full of flavor and worth the special trip. If you hop to, Victoria, and help me get these inside, I might even let you sample one."

I ran to grab a bagful. "You got it, Grandpa."

While we were still crunching on our apple wedges, Mom called. She invited Isadora and Mr. Wilkes for dinner, so the three of us trooped downstairs to the echo-y parking garage and climbed into the car.

In the dark, the windshield wipers slapped away the rain.

"We accomplished a lot tonight," said Isadora with satisfaction. She shot me a glance. "More than we expected, I suspect."

Mr. Wilkes's eyes met mine in the mirror. "We appreciate all the interest you're taking in the wedding, Vickie."

I looked out the window with a little tingle of quiet guilt somewhere in my throat. I knew I'd only been involved because I wanted to keep the ceremony from getting too wild. I had learned a few things. "That's okay," I said. "I haven't done much."

"Actually, I'm glad to hear you say that," Mr. Wilkes said. "Because we have another favor to ask of you."

"What?" I asked. "Whatever it is, I'll do it."

"We'd like you to write up something for our wedding invitation. Something original. Not clever, necessarily, but something that fits us."

Isadora interrupted excitedly. "We're designing it ourselves, and the printer will take it from there. But can you come up with any brilliant ideas?"

"You better believe it," I said, sitting back, ideas dancing through my head like the sugarplums did in " 'Twas the Night Before Christmas."

18

Dad was off cooking at the restaurant where he works, but Mom and Matthew were both waiting for us at home. Mom met us at the door.

"You're here. I'm relieved. The roads are so terrible."

I was very glad to see her, and I gave her a surprise hug which, of course, she returned. It felt good to be home.

There was a fabulous meal cooking away on the stove. Wild rice and baked chicken. Mmm. For a second I flashed back to the state fair and the poultry building, but I overcame it.

"Your wild rice dish is Chelsie's favorite," I said, leaning over the saucepan for a sniff. "What would you say if she came over?"

"I'd say, 'Where have you been all my life, Chelsie, old girl? Pull up a chair.' "

"Great," I said. "I'll give her a call."

"In return for my stunning generosity, can I count on the two of you to help with dishes later?"

"You bet."

I punched in the numbers. Fast. I get faster all the time, due to all the practice.

"Oh, hello, dear," said Mrs. Bixler.

"I'm calling to invite Chelsie to supper–if she hasn't already eaten."

"No, she hasn't, and I'm sure she'd love to come over. In fact, Mr. Bixler and I have dinner plans tonight. If it's all right with your parents, we could drop her off in about fifteen minutes."

"Beautiful," I said. "Thanks, Mrs. Bixler."

The doorbell rang. Chelsie was standing in the rain, getting soaked. "Could you give a starving orphan a good, square meal?" she asked in a pathetic voice.

"You've got your choice," I said. "Cold gruel or boiled cabbage."

She coughed weakly. "I'll take the cabbage." She came inside.

"You're just in time," I told her, taking her coat and hanging it in the closet. "Mom's dishing up a giant bowl of wild rice—all for you."

"Lead me to it."

We followed the delicious smell to the kitchen.

"Where have you been all my life, Chelsie, old girl?" Mom said without blinking an eye. "Pull up a chair."

We each grabbed a loaded serving bowl and carried it to the table. Then we gathered around like one big family and thanked God for taking care of us and for providing food. And for bringing Mr. Wilkes—Grandpa Wilkes—home safely.

"Matthew," Isadora said, after we had dropped hands, "why is it that every time I see you, you're wearing that same T-shirt? And isn't it getting cold for short sleeves?"

Matthew looked around the table, a small smile crinkling up his lips. "It's a secret."

"Come on, Matthew," I said, tickling him under the arm and making him jump. "Tell. Tell. You gonna tell?"

He nodded, rolling with laughter.

"Go ahead," Mr. Wilkes prompted. "Tell us."

When I let him go, Matthew caught his breath and explained. "At school they have this club. It's called the Tough Ones. We wear these T-shirts and hang out on the playground at recess. We tease kids who aren't part of the group, and we don't let them play on any of the swings or stuff."

Mom got red in the face and put her knife and fork down on her plate. We all knew what was coming. "That's outrageous!" she exploded.

My brother looked like he'd just had a bucket of

ice water tossed into his face. "It's just for fun," he said feebly.

"Fun! Matthew Mahoney, you know better."

Isadora and Grandpa Wilkes sat quietly. Chels was frozen in her chair.

Matthew's face scrunched, and I knew he was going to cry. Quickly, I looked down at my plate, because I knew that the last thing he'd want would be a lot of blubbering and sympathy. But I felt sorry for him, I really did. I looked at Chelsie across the table. Her face was serious, too.

Matthew had a lot to learn about life in general. I felt suddenly glad I had made it to eighth grade.

After dishes, Chels and I swiped a pomegranate and headed for my room. We had about a mile of paper towels, on account of pomegranates being notoriously messy. We sat cross-legged on my bed with the towels spread all around us and started picking out the little seeds with our fingernails.

After a while I said, "Poor Matthew. I bet he feels pretty crummy, especially after Mom said she was going to talk with his teacher. It's tough, being a little kid. He probably didn't even realize what he was doing."

Chels was smirking. "You old softie," she said. "You can be nice to your brother after all."

"Brothers are people, too."

"No!" said Chelsie, faking surprise. But I knew she understood.

The wind came up and whistled against my bedroom window.

"Hey," I said. "Do you want to help me work on the wedding invitation?" I had already filled her in on my new writing project.

"Write something down, and I'll be your critic."

"Okay, one sec. Let me think."

I started writing, pausing every little bit to look at what I had. I could hear her breathing quietly while I scratched out a few false starts.

"Time," she said after a while. "Tell me what you've got so far."

"Here goes:

"Come to the wedding of two crazy lovebirds, Isadora Shippley and Harold Wilkes. You've never seen anything like it and never will again.

"How's that sound?"

She snickered. "I like the stuff about crazy lovebirds. It fits. But it doesn't sound very serious. You need to add something serious."

I worked another couple minutes.

"Try this," I said and read:

"Witness their vows, and the beginning of their life together, with God at their sides and love in their hearts."

I stared at my handwriting in surprise. It sounded like a Hallmark card.

"It's perfect!" Chels said, grabbing the sheet away from me. "You've put their personalities right down there on paper. That's something. Congratulations; another wedding task completed. Now if you can just think of some way to get out of wearing the bull's-eye dress."

I filed the invitation in my desk and collected crumpled paper towels. I didn't say anything out loud, but I had already made up my mind about the dress. I would wear it without opening my yap even once to complain. I'd do it for Isadora and for my new grandfather. It surprised me to think I could be that unselfish. And it felt pretty good.

Bullrush, who is very fat and very orange and arrogant, emerged from under the dust ruffle and jumped onto the bed. Chels gave him a pet or two while I settled against the headboard with my back against a pillow. It was very quiet. Chels flopped onto her back and heaved a tremendous, bored sigh.

"Voila!" I shouted suddenly, just like Isadora does when she's made a discovery. Chels jumped into next week.

"What?" she yelled at me. "Why'd you scare me like that?"

"It just occurred to me what I can write that scholastic contest essay about. I'm going to write about individuality. You know, originality—being unique. I can start investigating it now, and then when the contest comes along, I'll be ready."

"You've sure got enough material," Chels said. "With Isadora and Mr. Wilkes and your brother and—hey, feel free to use my name. 'Chelsie

Bixler, Minneapolis resident, is one prime example of individuality in action.' "

"Cut it out," I said, pushing my stocking feet against her back so she rolled dangerously near the edge of the bed.

"Well," said Chels, "as long as you're so good at solving problems, want to talk about *my* problem?"

"Which one?"

"Guys. In general. As a whole."

"Save your questions. I don't have any answers." I suspected that some people were just naturally good at this sort of thing; but I wasn't one of them. Maybe I'd grow into it.

"I give up," Chelsie said at last. "This is one of those situations that I don't have an answer to. I propose that we both do the logical thing."

"What?"

"Pray. Consult God."

She was right. The problem was too big. I looked over at Chelsie gratefully. This was one of the great things about having a Christian friend. We could talk about stuff like this.

Chels screwed up her nose. "You want to know what my dad said? He said girls mature emotionally faster than boys, and that there'd be a few years' lag time before the guys catch up with us. Is that gross or what?"

"That's gross."

She yawned and added, "Maybe emotional maturity depends on the guy. I mean, like that friend of yours, Peter, he's not so emotionally immature or anything."

Peter was a guy I'd met in summer school before seventh grade—about a hundred years ago. I hadn't thought of him in a long time, being so wrapped up in Skip and Artie. Yeah, it was true. Peter was nice. And a guy, too. Maybe I'd give him a call.

I started a song, opera style, like Dad. "Oh, love," I sang, "you done me wrong! You done me wrong, wrong, wrong!"

Chels tried to smother my singing with the other pillow, but I was too quick for her.

"You know something, Vic?" she asked, when I finally got to the end of my song.

"What?"

"You're weird."

"Really?"

"*Very* weird."

"Thanks," I said. "I appreciate that."

JUST VICTORIA

I am absolutely *dreading* junior high.

Vic and her best friend, Chelsie, have heard enough gory details about seventh grade to ruin their entire summer vacation. And as if school weren't a big enough worry, Vic suddenly finds problems at every turn:

• Chelsie starts hanging around Peggy Hiltshire, queen of all the right cliques, who thinks life revolves around the cheerleading squad.

• Vic's mom gets a "fulfilling" new job—with significantly less pay—at a nursing home.

• Grandma Warden is looking tired and pale—and won't see a doctor.

But Victoria Hope Mahoney has a habit of underestimating her own potential. The summer brings a lot of change, but Vic is equal to it as she learns more about her faith, friendship, and growing up.

Don't miss any books in
The Victoria Mahoney Series!

SHELLY NIELSEN lives in Minneapolis, Minnesota, with her husband and two Yorkshire terriers.

AUTOGRAPH PLEASE, VICTORIA

Vickie Mahoney, celebrity?

The weeks before Christmas are exciting ones for Victoria. Winning a national contest brings attention from teachers, an interview on local TV, and a new excuse for best friend, Chelsie, to dream and scheme on Vic's behalf ("Do you want to hear my Vic Mahoney Promotion Plan?").

But Vic is distracted from her stardom by her little brother's big troubles. Matthew's "adjustment problems" in first grade turn out to be a learning disability. Once again the Mahoney family is put to the test, and once again their faith in God, affection for each other, and slightly crazy sense of humor help them survive.

In the process, Vic realizes a little more about who she is and what really matters.

Don't miss any books in The Victoria Mahoney Series!

SHELLY NIELSEN lives in Minneapolis, Minnesota, with her husband and two Yorkshire terriers.